THE 100% CURE

TO LARRY,

WISHING YOU 100%

HAPPINESS

Edward W. Hacer, MD

THE 100% CURE

Edward DeHaas, MD

Library of Congress Control Number:		2011913435
ISBN:	Hardcover	978-1-4653-4397-0
	Softcover	978-1-4653-4396-3
	Ebook	978-1-4653-4398-7

To order additional copies of this book, contact:
Xlibris Corporation
1-888-795-4274
www.Xlibris.com
Orders@Xlibris.com
102047

CONTENTS

FOREWORD

This novel is just that, a novel. Some may be alarmed by its content, but it's meant purely for entertainment and conversation. As with nearly any novel, it mixes fact and fiction. Names have been made up or, if possibly referring to a real person in my life, been changed. Names of prominent people or places may be the same. Any relation to real names is entirely coincidental, and no harm is meant.

Many events are, of course, based on real happenings in my life though, with artistic license, skewed to fit the novel. I have had a very interesting life, to say the least, and if I were to die tomorrow, I'd have no regrets. As anyone with any savvy can determine on the web, I've had a varied and often exciting life. I've actually traveled to many places in the world, been to war in Vietnam, have a Purple Heart, been married three times, graduated from Ohio State Medical School, worked in emergency rooms for many years, attended law school, and worked on American Indian reservations, among many other things, including three years in prison at Morgantown, West Virginia. Some of these events are reflected in this novel, but I can guarantee you that the facts may be greatly altered to fit the story.

I'm seventy-one now, and it's time for a new venture as an author. I really have no idea how the inspiration for this book came to my mind, but I thought it very entertaining. I do have many bizarre nightmares, which I attribute to horrible things that I saw in Vietnam. Oddly enough, they are rarely about Vietnam and often have crazy twists on the end as if they were preprogrammed. Go figure.

I feel that I am basically a good person, contrary to what you may think from this novel. I have always put the welfare of others before my own and try to treat people fairly. You can draw your own conclusions. It means little to me as I have a limited time left.

I would like to thank all my friends, relatives, and acquaintances for their input, contributions, and inspiration for my novel. My mother, who died from a stroke some years back, was always very encouraging and came to my aid even if I did something she knew was wrong. She always had a great sense of humor and took life as it came. My present wife, Connie, has always stood behind me in everything I do. I could ask for no more.

I hope you enjoy this book, and most of all, I hope it makes you think, think, think.

CHAPTER ONE

Time for a Change

After having worked nearly twenty-five years as an emergency doctor, I felt it was time for a change. So-called emergency medicine was getting to be a drag. Really very few true emergencies. Lots of colds, scratches, cuts, bruises, and things that would really take care of themselves without my help. Lots of unhappy patients waiting for treatment, lots of underpaid and overworked personnel. The bureaucracy was getting almost unbearable as was the paperwork and record-keeping. This was done largely to make money for the institution or company. Long hours often without eating properly and the accompanying sleep deprivation. Taking many continuing education classes that had little bearing on real life. Everyone thinking I'm filthy rich because I'm a doctor.

Well, I just couldn't hack it anymore. The physical and mental stress was overwhelming me. It interfered to a great extent in my social life. I had to come up with something different. I had lost all compassion and rationalized that I was doing little real good while reaping very few of the actual rewards. What I did observe was many wealthy people were receiving special attention and that money seemed of no concern to them. There had to be a way to capitalize on that observation.

And so my story begins.

Now I am no fool. I had seen numerous programs and read numerous advertisements and articles on "miracle" treatments and cures. The trick would be to lure very wealthy people into just such a plan. I felt, and still feel, that my miracle treatment would do no harm to any of the recipients and, at the same time, put me in the land of the rich and famous.

So in 1991, I set about with my plan. The first thing I would need, of course, would be start-up money. At the time, I was living in Youngstown, Ohio, working in the ER in one of the city's three large hospitals. One of the perks of my job was that they paid for my membership at the rather plush Brookshire Golf Club. I was a lousy golfer and didn't have a lot of time to golf. However, being the ER director, I was encouraged to join clubs and attend social affairs for public relations purposes. One Sunday in August, I was to attend a golf outing with some of the local wealthy dignitaries. As fate would have it, what great timing! One of the men in my foursome was Harold Thorndike, private owner of a very successful national trucking agency. I had become fairly close friends with him through prior engagements. He was a multimillionaire at a time when millions really meant something. He was also known as a humanitarian and a very likable person. He was in his seventies, and it is my belief that he really just wanted to be remembered. About the third hole of our round, a torrential downpour started, and we were forced back to the clubhouse. We sat alone in the lounge, sipping our beers and watching the wretched Cleveland Indians, of which we were both die-hard fans. What great timing again! Fortune seemed to be heading my way.

"Harry," I said, "I've been thinking about starting a cancer-research clinic."

"That's commendable, young man. And just how do you propose to do this?"

"I've been thinking a lot about this. I would like to make it some place classy, where people who have worked hard all their lives deserve the best."

"Sounds interesting. Go on."

Without hesitation (I had put some serious thought into this), I went on. "Like I said, I've been thinking a lot about this. My basic idea is to find a desirable location in Ohio. Once found, I'd build a luxurious housing development with a cancer clinic on its perimeter. With luck, the clinic could someday bloom into a hospital. The clinic would specialize in the treatment and cure of cancer. The housing development would initially help pay for the clinic. What I really need is some start-up money. I am planning on mortgaging my house, which is fully paid for, but realize that would not be nearly enough."

"And may I ask, how much would you get for your mortgage?"

"About $80,000 [a lot of money in those days]."

Harry promptly came back with, "That's not much for what you are talking about. You'll need upwards of ten million dollars."

"I realize that. It's just a thought of mine."

"Let me mull this over in my mind, and I'll get back to you."

"Great!"

The rain let up, and I let him massacre me for the last fifteen holes (I probably could have won a few of those).

Much to my surprise, exactly one week later, I got a phone call while I was in with a sniffling child. "A Mr. Thorndike would like to speak with you." I told the mother that I had an emergency to tend to and rushed to the phone.

Harry started, "Dr. Ed [that's what most called me], I've been thinking a lot about what we talked about. I think you have an intriguing idea. I am willing to put up one million dollars to get the ball rolling on this thing. However, you will be responsible for all of the legwork, and additionally, you have to promise to name the clinic after me."

"My very kind and generous sir, I don't think that will be a problem."

"Meet me in my office tomorrow morning at nine AM."

"Will do, bye now, gotta get back to work."

This was incredible. My dreams come true. I was at his office at 9:00 AM sharp, not a minute early, not a minute late. We discussed plans and paperwork and details.

Things moved quickly thereafter. I quit my job at the ER the following week and devoted the next three months to laying the groundwork for my idea. Harry didn't know it, but my plan was much more elaborate than his. Things were rolling along.

The next step was to find a location for my clinic. Harry was pleased with what I had done and told me he would pour in fifteen million dollars if things continued to look promising. Good old Harry!

CHAPTER TWO

Location, Location, Location

Now I am no fool. I may not always be right, but I am no fool. I had meticulously planned my course of action from the very start and would revise it as time progressed. The miracle cure started with dreams that began about one year before I quit the ER. It was as though a supernatural power were guiding me and telling me what to do. These dreams were extremely realistic and loaded with detail. The first step, now that I had some financial backing, would be to pick a location.

I had traveled quite a bit during my life. My father was an engineer who emigrated from the Netherlands. He had gone to the Royal Academy there and graduated with Queen Juliana. He kept getting better and better jobs. He even established several of his own companies. In the process, we moved quite often and lived in a number of cities in Ohio, Michigan, and Connecticut. I attended fourteen different schools before I was graduated from high school. At sixteen years old, with my parents' permission, I had joined the National Guard and, immediately upon graduation, went to basic training at Fort Leonard Wood, Missouri. They put me in the medics, so the last part of my training was at Fort Sam Houston, San Antonio, Texas. After basic training, I came back to college at Youngstown State (it was not a state university then) for undergrad and went to medical school at the Ohio State University. Afterward, I did my internship at Toledo Hospital. The day after my internship ended, I was back in the US Army on my way back to Fort Sam Houston for initial training to go to Vietnam. In August 1967, I found myself as battalion surgeon of the First of the Fifth Mechanized Infantry stationed in Cu Chi. On my return home from Vietnam, I was stationed at Camp Hunter Liggett in the Big Sur area of California. I then started my career as an ER physician in Cleveland and lived in a number of Ohio cities as opportunities arose. I stayed in the army reserve and went to a number of camps throughout the country. I traveled to many countries and United States destinations both on vacation and for medical seminars throughout the years.

When I returned from my army stint, I went to work at a brand-new hospital in Cleveland as their very first ER doctor. I continued in the army reserve for about fifteen years after, which will enter into my tale shortly. At the same time, I was going through a bitter divorce with my first wife. She had the papers drawn up and waiting for me on my return from Vietnam (some welcome home!).

Back in Cleveland and through the doctor that had the contract with the hospital for the ER (and I suspect made the money from it), I was led to the very wealthy and supposedly renowned attorney, Leonard Goldbergerstein (a remarkable name—everyone just called him Stein). Stein was a wiry little guy with a severe tic. He owned a huge yacht on Lake Erie and was a member of a yacht club there. He seemed to know what he was talking about. Therefore, I had hired him to take care of my divorce at huge expense to me. That's another story. This would be who I would contact to do our legal work.

I had gone to Akron University Law School in the early '70s on the GI Bill, but didn't like what they were teaching, so never pursued it. So what I am trying to get across is that I knew a little about the law. I was familiar with how things worked in Ohio, so I decided that was the place to open my miracle cure clinic and housing development.

In the early '70s, I was living in Canton, Ohio, and was in the 356th Evacuation Hospital of the army reserve. One summer—I can't remember exactly which year—we were to provide medical support for the NRA National Shooting Championships at Camp Perry near Sandusky, Ohio. I have always been a history buff. While I was there, I learned that Camp Perry was used as a POW prison during World War II for German and Italian prisoners of war who were mostly pilots and seamen. I started doing lots of investigating as I had a lot of downtime while I was there. We were actually housed in little cracker-box houses that held five prisoners and a potbellied stove. There were about 2,500 prisoners there, so I'm guessing there were about two hundred to three hundred of these huts still standing. They were kept in various states of repair as they were also used to house the NRA shooters every summer. The national championship had been held there every year since the early 1900s, and this post was the largest and most sophisticated shooting range in the world. There was only a small contingent of regular army stationed there to maintain the post, so access to the historical logs was easy. I found that, during the war, Camp Perry was used to rebore 105 howitzers. This was done by the prisoners. The train tracks in and out of the camp are still there.

As I said, during my downtime, I snooped around the camp where few have gone since the war. I saw the decaying old plant with rusted chains hanging down and the bunkers where they test-fired the howitzers over Lake Erie. The reserve doctors had lots of free time to travel to the surrounding area, and we stayed mainly around Sandusky. It seems that many of the Italians and Germans remained after the war and set up businesses in Sandusky, including a number of restaurants. We ate at great German and Italian establishments. I was able to meet some of the owners who were actually prisoners at Camp Perry and heard great stories from them. I learned that the Germans and Italians had no great liking for each other. This was reflected in the local politics, and Sandusky remained a dull and inconsequential place because of this. I had decided *this was the place!*

In the winter of 1991, I stayed in Sandusky for about two weeks, looking for the ideal location for the clinic. Harry was paying all my expenses and $2,000 a month until things developed. He also promised to put me up in one of the houses in the development when it was finished, so income was not much of a problem. After much investigation and conversation with the local people and real estate agents, I determined that Vermilion, a small affluent suburb of Sandusky, had much to offer. Some very wealthy families lived there, especially along the harbor. There was ample vacant land about a mile inland, which could accommodate the housing development and clinic easily. It was a quiet community with almost no crime. The mammoth amusement park, Cedar Point, was far enough away to keep traffic out. This was what I was looking for—a small low-key, affluent community.

I had spent a lot of hours scouting for a spot for our clinic and was worn out. I didn't have the wealth of information that the Internet provides today.

When I returned to Youngstown, I went straight to the phone to call good old Harry.

"Harry, how's it going?", I said.

"Couldn't be better! I hear you've been very busy."

"You must have great inside sources."

"Yes, I do."

"After a lot of work and investigation, I think Vermilion may be the place," I said, skipping the small talk.

"I'm very familiar with Vermilion. I had a small boat docked in the harbor there some years ago. I think that's a good choice. It's beautiful there in the summer."

"Great, we are agreed upon. Next, we'll need an attorney and a contractor to get started. Do you want to be involved in that part of the process?", I asked.

"Doc, I thought we agreed that you were going to do everything. I trust you to hire competent people."

"Thanks, I just wanted to know if you wanted input, sir."

"Please don't call me sir. We are business partners, and I'd like you to just call me Harry. Input isn't that important as long as you keep me abreast of things."

With more than a small amount of anxiety, I asked, "Yes, sir, just how free am I with the money?"

He became a little sterner. "Please don't call me sir. Look, I'm putting up fifteen million dollars, paying your newly acquired mortgage, paying your expenses, and giving you an ample amount to live nicely. Further, I'm going to put you up in one of those mansions you're going to build. I want this to be top-shelf. I want this thing to benefit people, but I expect some return out of it, too. I have complete confidence in you and want you to handle everything. Get the people you feel comfortable with. And by the way, I don't want the clinic called the Harold Thorndike Cancer Research Foundation. I want it to be called the *Harry* Thorndike Cancer Research Foundation."

"Yes, sir! Thank you, sir!" I replied, feeling pleased with his last statement.

"Please don't call me sir! And you don't have to thank me for anything. Now get back to work!"

"Will do, Harry!"

I hung up and turned to my wife, Connie, who had been listening in. "I think we're in business!"

"You've got to quit calling him sir and act like a businessman," she advised.

"Well, this is all kind of new to me. It's going to take a lot of long hours and days away from home," I informed her.

"Not a problem. I know you too well and support you all the way."

What a great wife! She probably knew me better than I have ever realized. After two failed marriages, I couldn't ask for more. She was and is as much as any man could ever want. She remains to this day a knockout—she could be a centerfold at seventy-one! She was Miss Ohio when she was twenty-one. Connie has quite a pleasant and reserved personality and is loved by everyone. She was a teacher and is very intelligent although I've had to explain every joke I ever told her. And to top it all off, she is constantly coming up with cute little games to play in bed. She puts up with me and backs me in everything I do even though she may not know what I am really doing.

"I'm now a businessman," I said, puffing out my chest.

"Yes, you are!" she said, with some reserve. "I don't think you really understand Harry. He is a wealthy and charitable guy. I don't think fifteen million dollars means that much to him though that is a terrible lot of money. I think you should adjust your thinking accordingly." Connie has always done a lot of charity work and probably understood Thorndike far more than I did.

"Good old Harry," I said.

"You better stop that!", she scolded.

I was exhausted after my trip and that phone call. After one of Connie's cute little games and twelve hours' sleep, I would call Mr. Goldbergerstein in the morning.

That night, I again had an amazingly realistic dream of detailed plans of things to come. These dreams were guiding me. All these plans were having outcomes with fantastic success.

At 9:30 AM, I called Mr. Goldbergerstein's office in Cleveland.

"Good morning. Attorneys Goldbergerstein and McIver. This is Rosy. May I help you?"

"Yes, this is Dr. Edward DeHaas. Mr. Goldbergerstein handled my divorce about twenty years ago. I would like to talk to him about another matter."

"He likes to be called Stein. He is not in right now. He is in court handling another of his million-dollar cases. He works way too hard, and I think it is affecting his health. He's driving me nuts."

This was way more information than I expected. I wondered if Stein knew that Rosy was giving out all these details. Regardless, she unknowingly was very helpful to me. I was pretty sure that I had this guy figured. Sure, justice was important to him, but not as important as the almighty dollar.

"Would you please have him give me a call?" And I gave my number.

"Sure thing, sweetie! He should be in late this afternoon."

"Thanks, I'll be waiting."

About five thirty, my phone rang. "Hi, Doc, this is Stein. What's up?"

"I really don't like calling you Stein. That is so ethnic. Would you mind if I just called you Lenny?"

"Not at all. So, getting another divorce?"

"Never, I've got a dream girl now. What I wanted to talk to you about was a proposition to handle a multimillion-dollar development I'm planning. I think it might be a great opportunity for you." I knew the mention of money would light him up.

"Sounds interesting. But let's not talk about it on the phone. Can you come up to my office this Saturday? Weekdays are tough. Say about seven thirty in the morning?"

What an ungodly hour, but who am I to argue? "Sounds wonderful! I think you might like what I have to say. See you then."

I figured that I would have to practice an outline of what we would talk about. I was quite sure that I would not have a lot of time with him. It was Wednesday, so I set to it. I woke at a very uncool hour on Saturday and drove up to downtown Cleveland.

As I walked into his office, I took in the very expensive black walnut paneling and many plaques of accomplishment mounted in impressive-looking handcrafted frames. Here was money! An attractive middle-aged woman sat at a desk that could have been a house for some lesser folks. This must be Rosy.

"Hi, you must be Dr. DeHaas. Stein's expecting you. Go on in."

"Just call me Doc."

I walked into an even more impressive room. It had a large conference table that must have seated twenty with a huge chandelier over it. Lenny was sitting at the end, going over papers. I needed some small talk to get us started.

"Hi, Lenny. Still doing the yacht stuff?"

"Sure thing. I have a ninety-two-footer docked up in Sandusky. How've you been? You look great."

Bingo! "Actually, I feel great. You look like you've been working too hard." This all fit in perfectly with what we were to talk about. But he really did look very tired and a little thin. His tic was worse than ever and quite distracting, but I chose not to draw my attention to it. His whole face went into contortions about every minute, and I was certain that he didn't need me to say anything about it. He was much thinner than the last time I saw him, and his skin looked a little gray. He was wearing an expensive suit, and I was dressed in my usual casual manner. I'm sure that made him feel a little more important, which is just what I wanted.

"Actually, Doc, I'm glad to see you. I'm getting tired of this rat race. Sure, I'm making tons, but I don't have time to enjoy it. It's ruining my health, and I just recently had an expensive separation from my bimbo of seven years. Do you have any suggestions?"

Bingo again! Skip the small talk. I was out-counseling the counselor! "You won't believe this, Lenny, but I may just have your solution. I'm planning to build a cancer-research clinic in, of all places, Vermilion. I have substantial backing from a millionaire to include an exclusive housing development adjacent to it. I'm planning on building about thirty plush mansions, clubhouse, golf course, and all. The homes will run from $300,000 to a million dollars each. [That built luxurious houses, to say the least, in those days.] We're going to need someone to handle the legal end of things."

We spent the next two hours going over details that I had prepared. I gave him pretty good answers to all his questions. I knew I was working on a budget, albeit liberal, so we had to negotiate. I was sure I had the right guy for this.

"I'm prepared to offer you one of the mansions, $200,000 per year, and 2 percent of the profits if you can commit to us exclusively. I know this may not be much compared to what you're making, but you'll live much nicer and probably much longer."

"You can't offer me 2 percent of the profits because it's supposed to be a charity. But I'll take care of that. Lots of charities make huge profits and just write it off as pay for labor. You know, I have lots of friends at the yacht club with money they don't even know what to do with. Vermilion is wonderful in the summer and an ideal vacation spot. I think I can get more than enough of them to put the money up front for mansions there as long as they have some say in building them. The money you speak of is peanuts to them. This would free up your capital for other things. They would enjoy summer homes near their vessels. Let me think this all over for a couple of weeks, and I'll get back to you posthaste. If I choose to do it, I'll need several months to get things straightened out here at the office. And, Doc, one of the first things you're going to need is a good contractor."

"I've got someone in mind. I'll let you know more after I talk to him."

This was more than I had ever hoped for, so I was anxious to get out of there before things might turn sour. Besides, that tic was driving me crazy. "Sounds good to me. I'll be awaiting your call."

We spent an additional fifteen minutes with idle chatter, and then I was on my way.

Two weeks later, I received a call. "It's a go!"

Another problem solved.

While I had been waiting for Lenny's call, I contacted an old Teke fraternity brother whom I had stayed in touch with and taken some vacations with since our days at Youngstown University. His name was Jimmy Contraro. He was from a Mafia family but never kept any close connections with them. He had a son named Wayne.

Wayne was a noted contractor who had been written up in a number of architectural magazines and had received many awards. He had to be about thirty-five by now and had done a little prison time over money problems. Word had it that he was back to active designing and contracting now and was still winning awards. Wayne and I had a lot of fun together when he was younger, about fifteen. I was about thirty years his senior and would always beat him at tennis. This always infuriated him because he liked to slam the ball, and I played little pop-placement shots—ran him all over the court. But we both always took it in good fun, and afterward, I'd take him out for pizza and a beer in a frosted mug. He loved sports and followed all the pathetic Cleveland teams. Through his dad, Jimmy, I found that he was now living in San Francisco. I decided to contact him.

"Wayne, this is Uncle Ed [as he affectionately knew me]. I heard you're in San Francisco and wondered if you'd like to try me again at tennis."

This brought some laughter. "Any time, Uncle Ed. I don't think you can beat me now."

"We'll see about that!" We spent about thirty minutes on the phone, talking over old times and making arrangements for my visit to California. It was decided I would stay with him at his estate.

So after the call from Lenny, my lawyer, I headed to San Francisco. Wayne had a spacious place there with an indoor swimming pool and a beautiful young thing in a bikini that had been staying with him for a couple of weeks. She was a real turn-on, but I can't remember her name at the moment. The first couple of days were just spent talking about nothing and playing a few games of tennis. I was now fifty-one, and he was in his late twenties. He had learned well from me, playing slow, sweeping serves and sneaky little drop shots. I still could have beat him but, of course, let him win. We had pizza and beer in frosted mugs afterward. This time, he paid for it.

After a couple of days of play, I came forth. "Wayne, my boy, I have a proposition for you that you can't pass up."

I went on to tell him the details of my plans for the cancer center and community development. If he came on board, he could lead a life of leisure. What a fool he would be to pass up an opportunity like this! He listened like a son to everything I had to say.

"Wayne, I can offer you one of the mansions, $175,000 per year, and a 1 1/2 percent bonus of any excess money brought in by this venture."

"You know, Uncle Ed, you have never given me bad advice. And it would be fun to live close to each other to play tennis. Let me think this over."

"Of course, Mr. Contraro. And please call me Doc."

"Please call me Wayne!"

Back to Youngstown. About a month had gone by, and I continued to work on the details. I was beginning to wonder if Wayne would call when, finally, the phone rang.

"Doc, I'm sorry I didn't call earlier. I had a little trouble with Trixie and had a hard time dumping her—you know how that goes. I've thought it over, and I'll be out there before spring is over."

And so it went. Everything was going smoothly, and everyone was going to be wealthy and happy. No one was going to suffer. What more could I ask for? What more could *we* ask for? Have to learn to talk like a businessman.

CHAPTER THREE

Lay of the Land

I spent the holidays of '91 at home because Connie always makes a big deal out of Christmas. Her two girls, my son, their spouses, and the grandkids (three little monsters) came; so a joyous time, indeed, was had by all. I never knew just what to get Connie for Christmas (or any other holiday, for that matter) because, like any man, I felt she had everything. But one thing I learned after three marriages was that every woman liked jewelry. Now I get her the real thing; but back in those days, when I didn't have a lot, I would go to the flea market in Hartville, Ohio, and buy her lots of jewelry. I had a knack for picking out stuff that looked real and expensive that only cost me a few dollars so I could buy quantity. I would get nice jewelry boxes to put them in so they would fool most people. She knew they were fake but loved them just the same. I am sure that she enjoyed the quantity more in those days than the few real things I get her today. Now that I think of it, I'm going to start going to the flea market again! Connie invented some great bedtime games during that break in work over the holidays. The one in particular I liked was "Ho, ho, ho!" She has names for all her games—she is so creative.

January 2, 1992, I was back to work on my project. I made frequent trips back and forth to Sandusky to get the lay of the land. I talked with businessmen, politicians, restaurant customers, and whomever I might glean some information from. About the third week into my sojourn, I was traveling on a farm road in Vermilion and saw a sign, "650 acres for sale by owner." Wouldn't that be great, plenty of land about a mile and a half from the shore in a low-key area? I looked for a house but couldn't find any. There was an old barn, though, so I pulled up the gravel drive and found an occupant.

This guy was something out of a book. He was thin enough to look ill, had a stubby beard, and was wearing shabby overalls and gloves with holes in nearly every fingertip. He came to meet me at my car and, as he approached, pulled up what looked like weeds and stuffed them in his mouth.

"Good stuff," he said with a slight German accent. "Loaded with flavinoids. My name is Tomas Strausser, but call me Tom. I suppose you saw my sign."

"Yup, you can just call me Doc."

"OK, Doc. You see, I have to sell my land to pay back-taxes. Why don't you come on in?"

I followed him into the unkempt barn as he picked a few more weeds and stuffed them in his mouth. It turned out that he knew the scientific names for all the plants on his property and seemed to know just what this and that was good for. It was actually interfering with our conversation; but I, of course, had to listen as though interested. The barn and everything around it were almost indescribable. There were rusted-out old cars, motorcycles, bicycles, and every appliance and gizmo you could imagine piled in and around the barn. Inside, the barn had a faint odor of urine and shit. Leafy stuff was piled on foam plates on a makeshift table. He was in the process of roasting a groundhog. He offered me some, but I declined.

He went on, "Sir, I have lived here since I was born forty-three years ago. My folks had a house up the road, but I quit school in the eighth grade and have lived in this great place ever since. I have about 150 acres of sod that I grow for the rich folks, and that has kept me going. I have everything I need right here. My folks were killed in an accident when I was sixteen, so I've lived and thrived here ever since. I never knew anything about taxes, and no one ever hit me up on it until about a year ago. Now I find I owe them $350,000, which I don't have, those bastards! To top it off, the weather with the lack of rain the last few years has ruined my sod. I really don't know what the hell I'm going to do."

I thought quickly. "Well, Tom, I might be able to help you. I'm looking for some land to put a development on. Maybe I could buy your land and help you out. Might even have work for you as a groundskeeper. But we'll have to clean up your treasures [I didn't want to call it junk] and maybe get you a little nicer barn."

We continued to discuss it and, between discussions on what to eat, came to a mutually acceptable agreement. I would buy the land for $560,000, rebuild his barn, and hire him as my groundskeeper. But we would have to clean the place up, and he could keep any proceeds from that. I didn't know it at the time, but between the scrap and things auctioned off, he got over $85,000. Good for him—he wouldn't know what to do with it. He was a very polite, likable, and intelligent guy though. So we made the deal.

I notified the proper politicians and authorities that the taxes were going to be paid off and, to no one's surprise, was welcomed to the community. I spent several weeks running back and forth to Cleveland for Lenny to do the legal work on the land. He set it up so that the homeowners would pay taxes (on very expensive property now), but the clinic, being a charity, would not.

In late spring, I gathered the troops—Lenny, Wayne, and myself. We met at the yacht club as Lenny was already a member, and it gave us all a chance to see the land and get a feel of things.

Lenny spoke first. "I've been very busy closing my practice and working on our project. I am quite certain that we can set the clinic up as a charity. I've been very successful recruiting potential homeowners. I've actually got sixty-seven who are, for all intents and purposes, committed. I didn't think we'd have enough resources nor land for that many, so I told them we are, for now, limiting it to forty. That caused a bidding war between them. I hate to give you the bad news," he said sarcastically, "but the bottom price of the homes will be $375,000 [huge back then]. They have all promised to sign papers to put the money up front so we'll have that money to work with. I want to treat them fairly. They want their input into the development of their estates. We'll keep only enough money to give us a modest wage and a little for good old Harry."

"You are something, Lenny. That's why I chose you. This is beyond my wildest dreams. I want to put in a plush clubhouse, golf course, tennis courts [a must back then], walking paths, and the works."

"Not only will we do that, they will be expecting it. Do you think you can handle this, Wayne?"

"I love challenges!"

"That's what I want to hear. When can we get started?"

Lenny and Wayne hit it off right away. They had both undergone divorces recently and were, as you would expect, horny. Lenny knew all the waitresses at the club and introduced Wayne to them—told him to take his pick! We all had great energy and wanted to get going as soon as possible.

Continuing discussions included the plans for the clinic. "My clinic is going to need a reception area, examining rooms, equipment and machines, conference areas, and at least twenty beds."

"Shouldn't be a problem, Doc, we now have about $14 million to work with."

They had seen the land and met Tom, the new groundskeeper. "We'll have to take care of Tom," I chimed in, which brought some chuckles.

Throughout the following year, we all worked closely together, always keeping each other informed and letting good old Harry know everything we were doing. We'd take an occasional break to spend with our families, and I took in a couple of Indians' games with Wayne, but mostly, we put in long hours. Lenny, of course, did most of the running around, satisfying the new homeowners and doing what lawyers do. Wayne immediately set out to hire local contractors for subcontracting. We wanted to keep the construction as local as possible for obvious reasons.

It was a good summer weatherwise, and the mansions rose rapidly. Beautiful paths and gardens were laid out. Tom did the sodding and, of course, had great suggestions on what to plant. A nine-hole golf course was laid out, complete with a luxurious clubhouse, pool, and tennis courts. We even had a sauna and massage room. Plenty of older trees of all kinds, many with blossoms, were left in place. Wouldn't Tom have a feast? I was kept busy planning the clinic.

By late summer of '93, people were driving up to their new homes in Mercedeses, Jaguars, Rolls-Royces, and whatnot. They were all very pleased. After all, they had complete input into the building process and knew they were getting a bargain for their money. Modest $250,000 houses were built for Lenny, Wayne, and me. An aesthetic twelve-foot brick wall was built around the entire development. The housing area and the clinic were walled off into separate areas, and both had posted guardhouses at their entrances. Wayne had thought of everything. He put in little touches that couldn't be found anyplace else.

He did a wonderful job on the clinic. There was a small plaque by the entrance doors that said "The Harry Thorndike Cancer Research Foundation." No signs were posted outside the walls. We had a spacious reception area, two exam rooms, an X-ray and nuclear medicine ward, twenty beds for inpatients, conference rooms—the works, all done professionally.

The list of homeowners was quite impressive. I was pleased when I saw a Buffett on the list, but it turned out that it was not "the" Buffett. This Buffett was a grumpy old man with an obtrusive and huge NRA decal on the back window of his Bentley. So be it—it takes all kinds. But we also had a lesser Rockefeller, a Dodge, and a Walton. Nice people! I have never had a lot of sympathy for very wealthy people even though most of them are pleasant people and have worked hard themselves. In one way or another, all of them have become rich on the labors of the not-so-well-to-do. Regardless, I felt it was my turn to be one of them.

Lenny specifically forbade any kind of homeowner organization in the purchasers' agreements. This was in case we wanted to expand on the ample remaining grounds, which, indeed, we did in later years. It was also so that the homeowners would have no influence over the clinic, which was the main purpose of our venture.

The sod brought in extra money for both Tom and us.

Surely, good old Harry was going to get his investment back and then some. But I shouldn't call it an investment. Legally, I guess, it was a donation.

Like Connie so wisely observed, Harry wanted the recognition more than anything.

By the spring of '94, the mansions were all occupied. Some were occupied by their owners, others by their housekeepers. Ninety percent of the owners would just use these houses as their summer residence. As it was bitter cold there during the winters, work on the landscape was pretty much limited to late spring, summer, and early fall. To this day, I do not see how anyone puts up with the winters in Northern Ohio. But the bitter winters played to our advantage by keeping outsiders away.

As the clinic was nearing completion, I had to bring on some doctors and ancillary help. I also needed some equipment. I started making lists to complete these tasks in the summer of '93. I made long lists of doctors, nurses, receptionists, of people I knew and didn't know. I really didn't want to advertise for help. I preferred to get people that I knew because I felt I was a pretty good judge of character. From the outset, I was going to treat the help fairly. I have always felt that if an industrious person is treated with respect and ample reward, he or she will give their all many times over.

It was time to do some traveling again to see some old friends.

Everyone was going to be happy and wealthy! No one would suffer.

CHAPTER FOUR

Gathering the Troops

One of the most important physicians our clinic would need would be a radiologist. After the process of elimination, I narrowed the list down to my first choice. I had graduated with Howard Cranston from the Ohio State Medical School back in 1966. We interned together at Toledo and were both called to Vietnam. We were in separate branches—he in the navy and I in the army—so we didn't see much of each other there. But after my stint at Camp Hunter Liggett, we both wound up in Cleveland. We had kept in close contact with each other for several years, then somehow drifted apart.

Howie (that's how I referred to him) chose to stay in the service and took his residency in radiology there. Through journals and annual Christmas cards, I knew he was still working in a large veterans' hospital near Washington, DC. Howie came from a small farm town in Southern Ohio and had that unique Southern Ohio drawl, which I fail to imitate. You can use your own imagination. He was a tall husky guy, and I could never, at that time, figure out whether he was gay or not. He didn't act gay, if that is possible, but he never took any serious interest in women. He did like to tease, though, and every time we saw a bush (as he called them), he would sing his little ditty to the tune of "Walk Right In"—"Walk right in. / Sit on my face. / Baby it's ah-no disgrace!" Howie had a saying for everything. He enjoyed doing basically nothing and would stack up empty cans of beer every night. However, he was very intelligent, and I can't imagine anyone not liking him. He was a lot of fun.

Through some effort, I found his home number (the Internet was not big then) and called him. "Howie, this is Fast Eddy. I've got some free time and would like to come out and see you." I got the nickname Fast Eddy from medical school when the movie, *The Hustler,* came out because people said that

I looked like Paul Newman, and I was pretty good at the pool table that we had in our recreation room.

"Damn, Fast Eddy, I haven't seen you since the pig had his tail straightened."

"Yeah, long time. You free this weekend, Howie?"

"I'm never free, but for you I'll make a two-for-one deal!"

So off I went to Washington. Howie wanted to meet me in a small sports bar. He probably didn't want me to see where he was living as it would be a mess. So I followed his directions and found him sitting at a booth in the back by himself, with a frosted mug of beer.

"Long time no see, Howie. Married yet?"

"Never fell into that trap, Fast Eddy. Got a bush coming in three times a week to clean my apartment though." God, he still calls them bush. I'd hate to be the one cleaning up after him.

With Howie, I knew we'd have to do some small talk first and gradually edge into what I had to offer. We first discussed what had happened since we saw each other last. Then we started telling stories.

I started about Vietnam. "Guess what, Howie. I had the solution to the war. I was in the Bobcats there, a mechanized infantry unit. We would set up in the style of the covered wagons with the '50s on the perimeter and support tracks in the middle. We were in the low flatlands in the middle of a peanut field near the Cambodian border. We were getting mortared every night. We knew it was coming from a little village near Cu Chi. I went into this village a couple of times a week on MEDCAPs with an armored platoon. We took care of the slant-eyes there and handed out meds during the day, which we knew were being confiscated by the Vietcong at night. Well, one day a Chinook bringing out supplies dropped off a whole case of Valium for some reason. I thought it would be a great idea to distribute this on our MEDCAP, knowing that the Vietcong would get their grubby little hands on it. Well, needless to say, we weren't mortared for several nights. So that's it—drop Valium!"

"You always were brilliant, Fast Eddy—smarter than Solomon's mother! Say, remember the time we were working together in the ER on April Fool's Day? Can't remember her name, but we convinced this hot young nurse to help us out with an April Fool's joke on the pathologist. We put her on a gurney and covered her up with a sheet and wheeled her down to the morgue. We told the bush that we were going to tell the pathologist that a body needed pronounced in the morgue, and when he would pull off the sheet, she would jump up and scream. She didn't know it, but the joke was on her. We just left her there between two bodies, and no one ever came down!"

"How could I forget that?" We laughed so hard that everyone in the place turned to look at us.

Finally, after a few more stories, Howie asked, "So what are you really here for, Fast Eddy?"

"You know me all too well. I'm opening up a cancer clinic, and I need a radiologist or roentgenologist, as you may prefer. Guess who I thought of?"

"You're keener than a Gillette fifty-blader, Fast Eddy. To tell you the truth, I'm getting tired of it here at the VA hospital. I've reached my maximum retirement, and it's time for a change. I'm lookin' for that blue horizon!"

"I know I can be up front with you, Howie. This may not be what you think. I plan on diagnosing and treating filthy-rich men for cancer when they really don't have cancer. I'm pretty sure it's all legal, and no harm will come to anyone. I'm tired of slaving away in the ER, and I've come up with a plan. If you're interested, you'll be compensated nicely."

I filled him in on the details. He would get a mansion with a housekeeper, of course, and a bonus. I would need him to bring a library of X-rays, etc., that showed pathologic processes. And I would need his help in selecting the appropriate equipment.

"Leave it to Fast Eddy. You always come up with neat crap. Sounds like you have something. I'm game. When do we start?"

I had him figured correctly. He would be a huge resource. He knew how to talk to people and was not a blabbermouth. He was as eager as I was. Howie could leave his job on short notice as he had overstayed his retirement. The only downside was that he would have to stay with me until his place was habitable. I wasn't certain how Connie would cater to his habits, especially knowing that she was Ms. Tidygirl. And she surely would not appreciate being called a bush though she wouldn't understand what it meant (I'd explain it to her!). Once, early in our marriage, Connie and I were flying on a plane, and there was this bitch of a mother constantly yelling at her very young daughter, who was actually behaving quite well. "Abby, Abby, Abigail!" Then it came—"It's time for an interactive moment!" I almost fell over laughing as the mom gave me a look that could kill. Since then, whenever Connie became upset, I would take her hand and say, "It's time for an interactive moment!" This invariably would change her mood. Well, this was definitely an occasion for a big-time interactive moment. After giving her a very cautious explanation of Howie and the temporary nature of his stay, she reluctantly agreed. What a woman!

My next step would be to find a genuine cancer specialist, a real oncologist. Over the years, I had been to enough seminars and met enough prominent physicians through my PR work that I knew a little about them. It was my view that many of the presidents of prominent charity organizations were in those positions primarily because they couldn't do anything else. Their lectures were boring and repetitive. They wouldn't know what to do if faced with a real patient. Many of them were that way, but not all of them. So I had to be a little careful. Once again, I narrowed my list down to one name, John Schantz (a nice German name!). He was president of a large charitable cancer organization and gave frequent lectures, a number of which I attended for continuing medical education. It was the same lecture year after year (I don't think he changed a word) about how they were investigating certain health foods that might cause cancer, like pears and iceberg lettuce and milk.

Dr. Schantz must have weighed about 350 pounds and was known as Porky, even to his face. Everyone I met who knew him spoke of him with great disdain. But he did speak with great authority and told good jokes. I would have to find out more about him. He was conveniently located in Columbus, Ohio. It would be nice to see what my old alma mater looked like!

I called him to make an appointment, and his secretary told me he would be available almost any time (he probably didn't do much). So I drove on down to Columbus, took in my alma mater, which I could no longer recognize, and strolled into his office. He was sitting on top of his desk with his legs folded, looking like Buddha reading a newspaper. He was in an uncomfortable-looking suit and tie and wore half-moon glasses, which he peered over with his head bent down. In a high-pitched voice, he said, "You must be Dr. DeHaas. Most everyone calls me Porky, which I don't mind for obvious reasons."

"I'm not calling you Porky. That is so disrespectful, Dr. Schantz."

"Whatever you please. What can I do for you, young man?" he asked politely. I was probably older than he was, but I didn't comment about it.

I spent the next couple of hours feeling him out and carefully explaining what I had in mind. I impressed upon him the importance of having someone of his stature (no pun intended) on our staff. There would be very little patient contact for him, but he would be used for consults.

He finally spoke up, "I think you and I both know that I am totally worthless here. I really need to change my lifestyle and lose some weight. I have no problem with what you are telling me. In fact, I have been thinking about doing something like that myself. As you spoke, I was coming up with some neat ideas myself. Being in the position I have been in, I can deal with rich people as well as anyone. I feel pretty much the same way you do about them."

That seemed to be becoming a universal theme. Does everyone think like that? Anyway, I explained the details to him and all the things we had already done. I told him we would build a house for him, a bonus, etc. I was speaking like a businessman. We spent the whole afternoon and most of the next day talking things over. He was close enough that he could stay in a motel (hopefully with a double bed!) until his place was ready. He came up with some great ideas that I had not even thought about. He, through his job, knew a number of wealthy people who had contributed to his charity and were always frightened of having cancer.

Porky (I called him that behind his back) suggested that, to hold down expenses, we could do a few things like getting phony research equipment and give bottles of normal saline with false labels on them—no harm to anyone. I was wondering how many doctors felt like we did. He took me to his house in Upper Arlington. It was a large, but modest, house for that area. He had a beautiful wife who looked like she was twenty but had to be older because they had four kids in their teens. He drove an old dirty Corvette, which he had to wedge himself in. Anyone could see that he needed a change, and he spoke my language.

We had an introductory meeting with the entire crew—myself, Lenny, Wayne, Howie, Porky, good old Harry, and last but not least, even Tom. We met in one of our new conference rooms of the newly built clinic. The only ones that knew what we were really going to do in the clinic were Howie, Porky, and myself; and that's the way it would remain. We discussed finances, operations, how things were progressing, and our future. Everyone—including Tom, who was cleanly dressed under my direction—had wonderful ideas. Howie, of all people, suggested that Tom get his rotten teeth taken care of! Lenny suggested his former secretary, Rosy, for a receptionist because he liked her work; and I told him that I would look into it. It was agreed that we would hire nurses to cover all the shifts, a radiology technician, and whatever aides, orderlies, and security people we might need. They would be paid well with full benefits, but of course, not the perks that we had. Lenny would handle their contracts, and all the docs would have to agree on their hiring. We would try to recruit them from people we had worked with. There would be no formal advertising as we felt that would look shabby to these wealthy patients. Security would be tight for both the development and the clinic for the patients' protection as well as ours. We would have intercoms to know who was coming and going.

Wayne would subcontract with his own helpers with Lenny's help and within a budget. Tom would do the same. Mr. Thorndike, bless his heart, was very pleased to see such progress and such cooperation. I'm sure he was also happy about the prospect of a little income. He told us that he was happy where he was and didn't care to live in the development. We decided that the word *development* sounded cheap and that we would, in the future, refer to it as *Vermilion Estates*.

It was made clear that the clinic would be entirely separate from Vermilion Estates in every way. Howie behaved himself well and was an entirely different and professional person when he was around other professionals. Porky pitched in with a few of his old jokes. Good old Harry's eyes lit up when he saw the plaque. So a lot was accomplished, and everyone left in a good mood. The docs would have their own private meeting the following day.

Howie, Porky, and I met at our clinic again the following day after a great night at our new clubhouse. We would discuss our initial plans. The building was nearly completed, and it was time to plan what we would do with it. We had twenty spacious private inpatient rooms with their own restrooms, each complete with Jacuzzi bathtubs and power showers. As it turned out, we never used more than five of them at a time, so we let some of our help sleep in them so they would look more occupied. We all had ample supplies of diplomas and certificates and licenses to hang on the walls of the reception room—very professional. Seems that my Purple Heart certificate drew special attention. Howie had a commendation from the president, whoever he was at that time. It was a regular museum of wall hangings and would occupy the time of patients while they were waiting.

We decided that we would not have our own lab—all specimens would be sent out (many of these, of course, were dumped over near Tom's barn). Unfortunately, the lab room had already been put in. We had a lead-lined room for genuine X-rays and, at Howie's suggestion, a large room for bogus machines. Howie had his own private room with a viewing board where he could review films with patients. I had my own private office with an Art Deco desk and decor, along with three examining rooms that would have mind-boggling equipment. We started drawing up protocols for every conceivable event. HIPPA, OSHA, and all the examiners would have to be dealt with. Fortunately, our status as a research institute and our security would help with that. We did all we could to make everything perfectly legal. Keep in mind that the three of us had always been the only ones to know what was actually going on at the clinic. All of us had great input.

Porky started, "You know, I already have a number of rather filthy-rich bastards that are great candidates for patients. I would like to suggest that we do routine exams on these pricks and try to determine which ones are gullible enough to be diagnosed with cancer and treated for it. Lenny and Wayne also know a lot of wealthy sonsabitches that could be clients. We'll have to be careful in our selections. Our candidates are going to need a clean bill of health. I know you can take care of that end, Ed, with Howie's help. We'll need a couple of more docs to make things look on the up-and-up, but we can get rent-a-docs [contract doctors] for those matters. They will have no idea what's going on. They'll all just be temporary, of course. I'd like to suggest that we import exotic tropical fruits and vegetables to supposedly use for treatment in our IVs, which we all know will actually just be normal saline. That way, outsiders who might see these packages will actually think we're using them for treatment. Maybe we could just serve them at our clubhouse. [That brought some chuckles.] I'll prepare the IVs with false labels so that the nurses will have no idea what they're giving the patients. Maybe we could warn the patients of some side effects from the medication. Triamterene gives a nice blue color to the urine and is a mild diuretic—won't hurt anyone. Good to have some harmless side effects."

Howie took his turn. "Sounds like you've done your homework. You've got more ideas than a porcupine's got quills! Anyone stupid enough to donate money to your organization certainly shouldn't take a lot of screening [brought a jiggling snicker from the Buddha]. I've been thinking about this a lot too. After the patient has been cleared by Fast Eddy, genuine X-rays will be taken to make sure all is clear. Then I'll take them in my private viewing room for consultation and show them films from my vast library. They'll be obvious films that any novice would be alarmed at. I'll tell the patient how only we have a surefire treatment for this. It will be important for Lenny to draw up agreements with any initial patients that, if they indeed are determined by us to have cancer, they will be treated by only us unless we direct them otherwise. In the case where they really do have cancer or come to us already diagnosed with cancer, after a thorough exam, we will tell them that we don't treat that type of cancer and direct them to the proper caretakers. We're going to need some fancy-looking machines that no one else has for our treatments. I know how to behave when I'm around patients. There'll be no bullshit. Just keep me supplied with brewskies [this brought another round of laughter]. I, as well you guys, want this perfectly legit. No one gets hurt." We could all tell that each of us had put a great deal of thought into this, and we were all very pleased and receptive of each others' ideas, with very minor alterations.

I contributed, "For sure, Howie. We have to make certain that nothing goes wrong. I don't think we're doing anything illegal, but no sense in taking chances. I don't think the HIPPA and OSHA inspectors will be much of a problem. I've had plenty of experience with them as an ER director. I've seen what the hospitals do. They always announce when they are coming, so there is plenty of time to get ready for them. I have a complete list of things they look for. They like to look at records mostly to see if you even have them. They just skim through them. I don't think they really look at them in any depth. They look for silly things like bottles stored under sinks and fire exits. We'll be prepared for everything. Like I said, I've seen what the hospitals do. You may not believe this, but the hospitals wine and dine these bastards, and I have even seen where they fix them up with some loose, hot chick who works in the hospital. You can't imagine what goes on. We can do that. I spoke with Lenny, and he told me that any of us can use his yacht most any time if we agree to pay his docking fee. During my snooping around here, I found a charter captain who is out of work because of the recent environmental warnings on Lake Erie. Maybe I could convince him to work part-time on the yacht. We'll cover that expense. Then we can get some bimbo to take care of these assholes.

You may not think much of Lenny, with all his nervous habits, but he is very smart and thorough. He won't know exactly what we're doing, but he'll cover us for every possible contingency. And he'll always be there if we need him for anything. He'll even take care of our taxes. No cheating on taxes—that leads to big trouble. He'll have his own office adjacent to the clubhouse. I really don't want him or Wayne or Tom hanging around the clinic."

The main content of our meeting was acceptable to all of us. We all had had enough experience in the medical bureaucracy to know the ins and outs. That was one of the main reasons we quit our practices, but this was our chance to trump the system. We spent another few days writing down our ideas and rehashing them until we all knew what each other would be doing. Wayne told me that he knew the perfect bimbo for our yacht, and I thought to myself, "Oh no, not Trixie!" Yup, it was Trixie. I thought this might be trouble but was willing to give it a try. We all agreed that we should get as little local professional help for our clinic as possible because we were all familiar with the blabbing that goes on from employees and the rumors that might be started. We wanted only pleasant rumors about our venture. We also preferred relatively young and inexperienced help in the clinic for obvious reasons that we didn't have to expound on. Howie knew some nurses in Toledo, about forty-five minutes away, and he would try to recruit them. Porky also knew some technicians and aides he would recruit from some small towns south of Sandusky. Tom and Wayne hired mostly local help, but these were largely temporary and had no direct contact with the clinic other than maintenance and grounds-keeping.

It was near Thanksgiving, so I took a little break and enjoyed one of Connie's games called Gobble Gobble. Then I headed for Avon Lake where Rosy was living. I met her at her home on a weekend when she wasn't working.

"Hey, Rosy, remember me? Lenny suggested that I contact you."

"How could I forget a handsome man like you, sweetie?" she answered, with her husband present.

I filled her in with what we were doing and offered her the position of receptionist. "We can offer you $16 per hour and full benefits including retirement, which is $4 more per hour than you're getting now. It's less than a forty-five-minute drive for you. I've driven by here a few times on Lake Avenue from Youngstown, mainly because I lived here when I was in sixth grade. We had a house right on Lake Avenue just where Miller Street hits it. I looked for the house, but it was gone. In fact the land was gone! It was nothing but wasteland when I live here, but I see now that it has developed into an expensive resort area." She was well aware of what I was talking about as most of the shoreline of Lake Erie was soft shale cliffs with one-hundred-foot drop-offs. It eroded quickly, and that was a long time ago. We found that we actually had some of the same teachers and knew some of the same people and had plenty to talk about.

"Well, Doc, that is a very nice offer, but I'm not sure I could work for Stein again. He was such a perfectionist and slave driver. I'm not too happy with Mr. McIver, his former partner, either."

"Please think it over. Mr. Goldbergerstein will hardly ever be around the clinic so that's not a concern."

"I'll do that, sure thing. How soon do you need someone?"

She called me the following week and said she would be pleased to work in our clinic. She was a little apprehensive because she was switching from a legal practice to a medical practice, but I assured her that should not be a problem. She asked when she could start. We had all agreed to try to open the clinic on February 1, 1995; so I told her that she would have plenty of time to get her affairs in order. She told me she had no affairs!

Shortly thereafter, I headed to the east side of Cleveland to the Spiker X-ray Company, a huge factory in an industrial section of the city. When I was working in Cleveland in the early '70s, I was doing some part-time work doing employment exams for the Spiker Company. I had to do very complete exams on the executives and, on one occasion, examined the CEO, Mr. Charles Westfield. When I did his rectal exam, we exchanged some off-color jokes and, later, became good friends. So I arranged to meet him in his office.

"Mr. Westfield, how's your rear today?" This drew a cynical cry. "I'm opening a cancer-research clinic over in Vermilion and am going to need an X-ray machine and film developer and whatever equipment goes with it, and I knew I could get your expert advice. That can be a major investment, and we want something that will last but not be too costly." So I told him what our needs were, and he advised me on the best machine and equipment, which I told him we would need posthaste. He had no problem with it.

"By the way, Charlie [that's what I had called him when we golfed together], we are also having some rather experimental and exciting treatment equipment being shipped in from South Korea. But we need something to house it in. I know magnetic resonance imaging equipment is rather a new concept. We basically need just the shell to house our ionizer. Any chance we could just purchase the shell on one of those beauties?"

"I'm not certain that will meet your needs, Doc, but I don't see a problem with it. It certainly won't cost you much just for the shell." And I was well aware of that.

The horrendous winter that year halted any outside activities, but fortunately, nearly all the outside projects were near completion. Finishing touches were done on the insides, and we completed our initial recruiting efforts. We were getting a lot of brand-new equipment in which we all pitched in for "some assembly required." Our X-ray machine was installed complete with all its frills. In a separate room, which was not lead lined (that was expensive), was installed the shell of the MRI machine. Privately, the other two docs and I experimented with various devices to make impressive sounds. We tried buffers, sound recordings, hair dryers, and other devices. We finally settled on a cheap food blender that, when rapidly turned off and on, sounded very authentic.

Howie was very handy with electrical gadgets, so he rigged it up so that it would quickly alternate—on, off, on, off, etc. He also installed an eerie blue light that would come on when the machine was running. It was placed inside the shell. No one would enter this room except Howie because, after all, it was secret experimental equipment. Wayne, also being an electrical engineer, would have been of great help with these devices but, of course, could not be let in on our top secret experimental equipment. Howie also devised several impressive-looking gizmos that lit up and made noises but did absolutely nothing. One device even had a large control board that took up half a wall in the room that was initially going to be our laboratory.

Christmas and New Year's Eve passed with Connie's usual innovative games, which I enjoyed immensely. You really don't even want to know some of the names she made up. Some of those names alone were enough to turn you on.

Everyone was going to be happy and wealthy. No one would get hurt!

Chapter Five

Get Ready, Get Set

It was early January 1995, and our opening date for the clinic was anticipated to be February 1. Some panic was setting in as might be expected with any opening business. We all had plenty to do yet and started to put in long hours. We were all wondering whether we would have enough patients to support the clinic. I suppose that is something that goes through the mind of any entepreneur.

Vermilion Estates was not much of a problem. Wayne had completed nearly all his work. His house—along with Lenny's, Howie's, Porky's, and mine—were about ready to move into though not quite finished on the inside. Our houses were in a separate section on the perimeter of the complex. This was done purposefully so as not to distract from the opulent palaces in the main area. Ours were quite attractive by any standards, but not to the extent of the owners'. It turned out that all the owners had tried to outdo each other. Tom had put in beautiful lawns, gardens, paths, etc., to make the grounds look like something from Eden. He was nearing completion with his work on the estates. The clubhouse and ancillary buildings still needed quite a bit of labor to finish. Minimum property for each titleholder had been set at two acres by Lenny, so we still had a significant amount of land. We had had enough demand for the properties that we could be exceptionally selective. We didn't want any owners who were medical professionals, for understandable rationale. Because of the age of the owners, no kids were to be seen except for Porky's and, occasionally, some visiting grandkids. Background checks were done on every family to make sure there would be no troublemakers. Eight of them became regular patients at our clinic. Two were Arabs who had acquired their wealth from the oil business. This turned out to be a favorable omen as there would come a time when the buyers would be nearly exclusively Arabs. Twelve of the owners belonged to Lenny's yacht club. We expressly excluded any local citizens from ownership because we didn't want gossip floating around the area. As already stated, the local politics were competitive enough to keep the elected officials busy with other matters. Our security guards were to follow strict guidelines for the owners' protection.

Assets were not, in truth, a considerable concern but could be if the clinic didn't deliver.

The estates had all been paid for in advance, so that didn't deplete our financial arsenal at all, except for a little over a million dollars for our personal houses and Tom's new barn. The clubhouse and secondary structures were all figured into the intial costs of the owners. After expenses for the clinic, equipment, and initial wages, we were down to a little over seven million dollars. The good news was that we had cleared something over half a million in interest during the preliminary work. Lenny was a wise investor. We would probably need every penny of this if our plans were to succeed. Lenny saw to it that, because of our charitable status, taxes—other than our personal taxes—were not much of a problem. And he would take care of those, too, knowing every legal loophole.

Our support services were hired on early so that we could all be on the same page. We needed their help in putting final touches on things and readying the clinic for opening day. We had to make certain that they knew the right things to say, know how we operated, learned and helped with protocols and algorithms, and be in the right place at the right time. They had to be cleared for security and know our security policies. We had to get to know them and what we could say around them. A lot to do in a short time. Each had to be interviewed by all three docs so that we were all comfortable with them. We had regular meetings, both privately and in goups. Personality was everything. True to his word, good old Harry stayed out of everything. About the only time we ever saw him was to keep him abreast of our great progress and to reward him with a small return.

Wayne, Lenny, the other two docs, and I had a long private meeting to discuss our finances.

Lenny, our attorney, began, "Look, I think you guys would be fools to have set fees. I think you should just ask for donations. These guys have so much money that they light their Cuban cigars with C-notes and throw expensive crystal wineglasses in the fireplace after they finish their vintage wine. I am willing to bet that they'll donate a minimum of ten thousand each."

I replied, "That's fine and well. But we only ask them for a contribution at their initial exam. The money will be in the treatment, and we'll have to charge for that. Most of these guys will already be up in years and will want to extend their longevity. After all, that's what they will be there for."

"I don't see a problem with that, and I believe that they'll believe that is a reasonable thing to do. I agree that the treatment is where the money will be. We're not going to take insurance, and our explanation will be perfectly plausible. Medicare is fraught with government inspectors and nothing but trouble. We are doing experimental, although be it curative, work. We take only cash, check, or credit cards." We all agreed to Lenny's advice.

I changed the conversation. "I think we should let Lenny handle all the money. He has done very well for himself in the past and has more than all of us put together. He has done well investing our money. He'll have plenty of time on his hands once we get going. I don't think we should have any kind of secretary snooping into our finances. I trust him fully."

"I'm flattered by that. I don't think that will be a problem with me. I'll have a complete financial statement of everything that comes and goes every three months. I can handle the payroll also. This OK?"

Wayne, our architect, said, "OK with me. We're all in this together, and the docs seem to have some kind of miracle cure."

"OK with me," replied Howie.

"Me too," said Porky, trying to get comfortable in the standard-sized chairs we were sitting in.

So our financial affairs were settled after going over a proposed budget. It seemed like this part of our endeavor would be relatively simple and straightforward. Lenny would also take care of everyone's personal finances at their request; and no one, not even our help, would have it otherwise. We could only take his constant squinting so long, and the meeting adjourned.

All the interviews of the medical personnel were done privately with just the prospective employee and the three docs. The first interview was with Rosy and went smoothly. She called everyone sweetie, and she was cheerful and showed great appreciation for what we were doing. It was hard not to like her. She pitched in with everything and knew just what to order for the front desk. She was given copies of our protocols and algorithms and instructed to learn them thoroughly as she would be quizzed on them. We did this with all our employees and included ourselves. If we expected it of them, we should be on the same page. We had different modus operandi for each position. Rosy was pleased that Stein was nowhere to be seen.

Our next meeting was with our future X-ray technician. All the docs introduced themselves, and then she spoke in that distinctive Ohio farm-girl twang, "Hello, y'all. My name is Helen Savorsky, and I am almost twenty-two years old. I am so pleased to meet y'all. Dr. Cranston found me through a technician he had worked with that recommended me. I have completed my training at Toledo Hospital and am fully certified and registered. I've worked for six months in Clyde, where I live, and am quite frankly looking for a better-paying job like you are offering. I can start immediately."

We could tell at once that she had rehearsed her introduction perfectly. She was as cute as could be. She was petite and well put together. She wore a pleasing V-neck top that showed just enough of her cleavage to make us want to see more. She had youthful bouncy breasts that were neither too large nor too small. She had a smile that would make you melt. She walked very sensually, with a side-to-side farm-girl gait. We all were quite delighted with her.

I responded, concerned a little over her brief experience, "Let me tell you a little story. When I was in Vietnam during the Tet offensive, we captured a North Vietnamese soldier who looked to be all of sixteen years old. He willingly told our interrogator what had happened to him. He was brainwashed to believe that his mission was more important than even his life. His mission was to carry two mortar shells in burlap bags for several hundred miles down the Ho Chi Minh trail. He told of how many of his comrades had been killed by our B-52s and how he spent many hours in swamps, breathing through a bamboo straw. He lived on a bowl of rice a day. When he got near Saigon with his two mortar shells, he handed the first to another soldier who was firing them off. The other soldier fired the first shell while he was fetching the second one, so he missed seeing the first one shot off. He was so infuriated that he hit the other guy over the head with the second round and knocked him unconscious. He then surrendered to our troops. Think about that. He went through all that, and in the mind of a young kid, didn't get to see the final outcome. We don't want anything like that to happen here."

"Dr. Cranston gave me the protocols and algorithms that y'all prepared, and I have studied them and nearly memorized them. I realize that what you are doing is largely experimental and new. I understand that y'all have had great success with cures and think that is peachy. I know what my duties will be and that I will be limited to that. For good reasons, I ain't going into any secured areas, and I ain't got no problem with that. One thing, though. I admit that I smoke. I saw nothing on the smoking policies."

One could see that this girl (or bush, as Howie would call her) was on the ball. To be sure, we had not put that in the protocol, and it would have to be added. I comforted her, "Times are changing. More and more medical facilities are banning smoking. To make you feel more at ease, please know that all three of us smoke. Dr. Shantz smokes at least three packs of Camels a day. We have always smoked right in the hospital while doing our charts. But like I say, times are changing, and we have kept up with that. Mr. Contraro, our contractor, has kindly put a small room at the back of our clinic for this purpose. It is fully ventilated with up-to-date, sophisticated equipment. You will be able to take smoke breaks whenever you are free, but don't abuse the privilege."

"Sir, I would be a fool to do that. I know what is expected of me." Indeed, she did. She would always be one of our favorite employees.

The next scheduled time was for a nurse for the outpatient part of our clinic. He was a male nurse who showed up about fifteen minutes late. During our questioning, he gave us the impression that he wanted everything his way. He had all sorts of ideas for us that we, in actuality, had no need for. He wore a white uniform that had some small old blood stains. He admitted that he was having a problem with a girlfriend (he was married). Needless to say, he was never asked back.

The following interview was with a nurse for the same position. She was a sharp, well-dressed gal in her early twenties. She wore a turtleneck that actually did not deter us from gazing at her voluptuous boobs, though I'm certain that it was meant to because her personality was sedate. She was single and had no hang-ups. She wore a conservative cotton suit jacket and carried a small briefcase—I'm sure for her to look businesslike. She too had reviewed the procedures. She spoke like a well-educated person and with exceeding graciousness. We again introduced ourselves.

"My name is Stephanie Dickenson, I am twenty-three years old, and I live in South Amherst, which is an easy drive from here. I want you to know that I am fully licensed and registered and up-to-date on my continuing medical education. I completed my nursing education at Sandusky General and am presently working on the coronary-care unit at Norwalk Community. My primary incentive in the job you offer is to take part in something that is groundbreaking. The money, which is considerably more than I am making, is important, but to me, working in a place like this is even more important. I've read your protocols and understand them. I will be thrilled to work with such noted physicians as yourselves."

Howie stopped her. "You talk like you've already got the job! Can you start soon?"

"Tommorow, if you wish." We didn't even have to think twice about her. She would come to be known as Stephy. I told Howie to dare not call her a bush!

We still had planned interviews for two full-time professionals to cover the inpatient part of the clinic. They would have to work twelve-hour shifts, and it would be important that they were in harmony with each other. As it would turn out, we would never have more than five inpatients at a time, so there wouldn't be a lot for them to do. Weekends and breaks would be covered by part-timers. There would be a daytime aide for appearances only. These two nurses could make their own hours between themselves.

The first that we would hire was a stocky, large-boned woman who looked about thirty. She was clean, in a bright white uniform and wore a nurse's cap, a thing that was disappearing. She was a little overweight and plain looking, but her energetic style and beaming facial expressions made her attractive. She took off her snow-covered shoes before she sat down.

"My name is Judy Gomez. I didn't want to mess up your pretty new carpets. I hope you don't mind—I bathed my feet this morning. I live in Fremont, home of President Rutherford B. Hayes—not too far from here. As your background checks will show, I have all the qualifications necessary for the job. I haven't worked for about six months due to illness in the family, so I am ready to start any time. I've familiarized myself with your policies and have no problem with them. I know how to keep records, so that should be a plus. I'm not married and have no children. I have a live-in boyfriend who is doing well in the landscaping business. I have a twin sister who is also a nurse and looking for a job, but she somehow got overlooked by you."

Porky halted her there. "Would you mind if the three of us stepped into the other room?" She looked a little shocked but, of course, agreed. The other two docs and myself went back to have a smoke.

"That was a little rude of you to interrupt her like that, Dr. Shantz."

"Well, she may turn out to be pleased. I like her, and if she has a sister that is anything like her, that would make a good pairing. We've all worked in hospitals enough to know how one shift is always complaining about the other shifts. We don't need that. I say that we hire her and interview her sister tomorrow."

We all agreed to that. When we returned, Porky explained why we had our little private conference, and we could see that she was much relieved. She said that she was a little worried about what we had to say about her until it was explained. Porky, gentleman that he was, apologized. She was quite receptive to having us check out her sister the next day.

They were supposed to be identical twins but looked and acted more like fraternal twins. One might even guess that they actually had different fathers. Jody, Judy's sister, was the same height as her sister but was much more slender and outgoing. She had an excessive amount of makeup on and wore lots of expensive-looking jewelry such that I was used to buying at the flea market. She had an exaggerated wiggle when she walked. Her high heels were *very* high heels. She was definitely on the hunt. She talked in an educated manner much as her sister did. We had done a quick background check on her and found everything to be what we needed. The thing now was to find out how she and her sister got along.

"Hi, I'm Jody Gomez, Judy's sister. I live only two blocks from her in Fremont. I trained right along with her and have similar qualifications. I don't know how it came about, but you can see that we are quite different. But two sisters could never get along better. If either of us is in need, the other is always there to help out. We know virtually everything about each other. I hope that will not be a problem. We are both quite discreet and never talk about patients except to each other. I understand that you hired my sister, and I would be pleased to alternate shifts with her. Do you mind if we occasionally work twenty-four-hour shifts so that we can switch days?"

I answered, "Not at all, just as long as the ward is always covered when we have inpatients. You talk like you are already hired, and I believe, if it is all right with the other two docs, you are [they nodded their heads affirmatively]. You will have a daytime aide when you start your regular duties. We don't anticipate having any inpatients for the first few weeks, but there is plenty to do, so you can both start any time. You can even help out front when we open. You'll like Ms. Savorsky and Ms. Dickenson and our receptionist, Rosy. Whenever there are no inpatients, only one of you will have to be present just during the day, and you can help out up front. Any problem with that?"

She, of course, complied. We suggested that she dress down a bit, and she told us that she dressed in uniform for work and didn't wear jewelry because it was a hazard. Great!

Trixie would not come until the warm weather when we would need her. We all had reservations about her, but that would be settled when it came time to interview her. We would pay for her trip from California.

So our professional staff was organized, and we went immediately to work preparing forms, assembling equipment, and practicing protocols. Lenny would do a final review on all our forms to make sure that they were legal. There were forms that explained to the patient that, given the diagnosis of cancer, they would follow exclusively with us. They would all be given the standard HIPPA forms explaining their rights. These were altered slightly to conform to an experimental situation. We kept Lenny away from the clinic as much as possible both because of the slight conflict with Rosy (though he recommended her) and because his tic was very wearing on the nerves. We all agreed that we would have dry runs for several days prior to our opening. The docs would act as patients but also have their own practice sessions among themselves.

Howie and I liked to inject some humor to ease the anxiety. We told stories that had happened to us through the years. We could both remember the joke we played on the chief resident of obstetrics and gynecology (OB-GYN) during our internship. There was another intern that we called Travis (he said that was his taveling name!). Travis dressed up like a woman—lipstick, wig, perfume, and all. He looked for all the world like a female. He presented himself to this resident as a patient. The nurses were all in on the joke. He first gave his history of severe itching in the private area. Naturally, the nurse prepared him for a pelvic exam with a sheet draped across him. In the meantime, this resident was telling us about this weird woman. We did all we could to keep from laughing. So he went into the exam room and lifted the sheet, and you can imagine what he saw! Our girls all laughed at this story, but I'll wager that they were concerned about what kind of pranks we'd pull on them. But that never happened except for inocent little capers when patients weren't around.

It was reiterated again and again about how we had to keep everything confidential to protect our experimental work. We told them that we would go public with it once we were certain that there would be no problems. The staff was expressly forbidden from entering any of the doctors' offices or the room where our classified equipment was kept. This machine would become known as our NNI. It would be called that by everyone except to any inspectors that might come around, in which case it would be called the negative-neutron ionizer. The doctors were not to be disturbed except for extreme emergencies. Our phones were all screened by a system that would detect any bugging. Computers were not in prominent use in those years, so we didn't have any.

All were present for our dry runs, except for when the docs had their own restricted rehearsals. The last days of January arrived, and we hunkered down to these rehearsals. It was near zero degrees; and the dreaded "lake effect," which was the bitter cold winds blowing off Lake Erie, was in full bloom. It was blizzard conditions with the snow piling in huge drifts, making traffic hazardous, but somehow, everyone made it on time to our meetings. Much thanks to Tom, who plowed the roads and walks in our complex. Wayne was busy with his crew, putting finishing touches on the inside of buildings. Lenny was occupied, going over forms that we formulated. The docs, as I said, would act as patients and ask difficult questions and pose difficult situations. Everyone knew the importance of confidentiality, especially since we were doing secretive experimental treatments. We were confident from the interviews and background checks that the girls would behave in a professional manner, and there was never any problem with that.

Our first tryout was for the initial exam in the outpatient part. Locum tenens specialists like the cardiologist and proctologist had not yet been taken on, and they would be briefed on their arrival. They were to arrive on opening day. All initial visits were to be complete exams to make certain the patient was in good health, or in the alternative, to find "cancer." If they were found to have any genuine serious disease, they would be referred out. We would take care of any minor problems as we were all qualified to do that. The first visit would include a very thorough history, a chest X-ray, a stress test, a colonoscopy, comprehensive lab studies that would be sent out, pulmonary-function tests, and of course, a discussion about the need for contributions. Acquired immunodeficiency syndrome (AIDS) was a fairly new thing then, but we were concerned about it especially in light of the fact that Trixie would soon be coming up from California. It was a very expensive test in those days, but we would absorb the cost. As it turned out, some patients actually came to us with cancer. After the exam on these patients, we would simply tell them that our treatment was not effective for their type of cancer.

I would be the first patient. I was escorted into the clinic by a cheerful security guard who promptly left. Rosy was at her desk, and the others were at their stations.

I started. "Howdy doody, my name is John Doe, and I'm here to see Dr. DeHaas for my exam. OK, Rosy, your turn."

"Welcome to our facility. My name is Rosy. You will first have to fill out some legal forms and supply us with your complete medical history. The doctor will review them before he sees you, so you'll probably have to wait a few minutes. As you will see, there is plenty in our waiting area to keep you entertained if you wish. If you have any questions at all about these forms, please feel free to ask, and if I can't answer them, I'll let the good doctor know. There is no fee for your visit, but we would appreciate any donation you can give. It's all tax-deductible. Any questions?" she said with a sweet smile.

Trying to be difficult, I came back a little gruffly, "I know what 'a few minutes' means—been through that before."

"It will only take as long as it is necessary to go over your history. It is for your own well-being. We schedule our appointments so as to make the wait minimal."

"An excellent comeback," I told her.

At this point, I had Stephy ring the fire alarm just to see how well everyone prepared. But I was kind enough to tell them only to pretend to go outside because of the weather. They all did exactly what they were supposed to, and it gave a little humorous relief.

We continued. "That really wasn't so bad, filling out those forms. Where it said 'Sex,' I put 'Yes'!"

Though a little offended, Rosy replied, "That's very humorous, Mr. Doe. I'll call the nurse to take your vital signs."

And so it went, from checking in to checking out. Stephanie took my pulse, blood pressure, respirations, and pulse ox, and then prepared me in a gown for my examination. Helen pretended to take my chest X-ray. Howie pretended to review it with me. Pulmonary-function tests were actually done, as was a stress test, to familiarize everyone with the equipment and procedures. I posed some rather tough questions to the girls, and they all gave satisfactory, if not superb, answers.

When we were through, I said seriously, "I would like to donate one million dollars to this fine facility provided, of course, that a plaque be made up for me for the lobby."

Jody quickly returned, "I don't think that will be a problem!" And we all broke out in laughter. We were one big happy family, and that's what everyone wanted. We all went for dinner at our unfinished clubhouse where we had a local chef from a popular German restaurant in Sandusky, Die Elende Frau.

We repeated this ritual the following day and the next and the next with everyone adding their suggestions. We had some brilliant minds at work. Despite the wretched weather, everyone was always on time and anxious to do the real thing.

We docs had our own separate meetings and not only did dry runs but went over our strategy.

"What if the patient decides to go elsewhere for treatment? Don't you think that will be a problem?" I questioned.

"Au contraire," said Porky, trying to be coy, "they will have signed a contract with us, and it will be up to the three of us to guarantee them that they will only get a complete cure if they follow exclusively with us. No one will get hurt." Howie and I were both glad to see his confidence, and we agreed with him.

Howie joined in, "All right, Ed, you will first do a comprehensive exam on the patient, and then you will direct the candidates for treatment to me. Then I'll have a compassionate discussion with them in my private viewing room and show them a film from my extensive library, showing them an obvious disease process. And I will impress upon them the importance of following only with us for treatment as we have had a 100 percent success rate. They'll then be introduced to Dr. Shantz who will direct them on treatment, which will include our 'blender', or negative-neutron ionizer that you might call it. Let's all refer to it as the NNI around our help. I'll handle the operation of that. No one comes in that room but me. Then to compliment that, Dr. Shantz will admit them as an inpatient for very expensive IVs. He'll explain to the patient how we must get exotic tropical plants for the contents of these fluids. I think we should just charge what we feel comfortable with for the treatment. These assholes have money coming out their ears. If hundred-dollar bills were a grain of corn, they'd have a farm. They'll be happier than a cock in a henhouse!"

Porky replied, "Yup, that's about it. I think we should get comfortable for a couple of weeks just doing the exams before we start a treatment. We'll have to screen our therapy patients carefully. We don't need any know-it-alls or snoops or loudmouths. We'll be able to feel them out during our conversations and by reviewing their personal histories. You must realize that all these patients will be coming to our clinic for a clean bill of health, and in the alternative, they will be convinced that we are the best. Any problems?"

I answered, "I think we're all on the same page. Now let's do a dry run amongst ourselves. I want you to think of the toughest questions you have. I'd rather be prepared for things than run into problems when we start for real."

We practiced over and over again until we were all talking the same language. We thought of every possible contingency. We would ask Lenny for help on legal problems, but he would always believe and advertise that we were miracle doctors.

Lenny had eight patients lined up for us to start, Howie had two, and Porky had twenty-four. I knew of three from my PR dealings.

The big day was near. Everyone was going to be happy and wealthy! No one would get hurt!

CHAPTER SIX

Go!

It was the eve of February 1. We completed our last dry run and had six patients lined up for our first day. However, the weather was brutal. It was below zero degrees, and the snow was piled up into over four-feet drifts. All our girls decided to stay over and sleep in the wonderful rooms of our inpatient section rather than risk the weather. We had food brought to them from the clubhouse. We were all apprehensive about having any patients at all on our opening day. Howie, Porky, and I struggled over to the clubhouse at about six thirty for a last-minute briefing. Howie ordered the local German beer, Gift Wasser, and a cheeseburger. Porky, like a good boy who was dieting, had a chef salad and Bud Light. I, with all my anxiety, was not very hungry and just had a grilled cheese and draft.

After we had all settled down and eaten, I began. "I'll be surprised if we have any patients tomorrow with the weather—a shitty start. Looks like we'll have to be here just the same on the chance anyone pops in."

Howie responded, "Nothing we can do about it. It's snowing like the ashes of St. Helen's! We've got six patients scheduled for our first day, and it will be a miracle if we get any. I'd like to get at least one, though, because we need the practice."

"I hope I don't need to say this again, but let's be careful selecting our candidates for treatment. It doesn't look like our locums docs are going to make it in, so we'll have to skip the stress test and colonoscopy if anyone shows up. With that terrible prep for the colonoscopy, if we have to repeat it, that won't make anyone happy. Good thing there's no charge for the initial exam," Porky joined in.

I changed the subject. "Look, you guys, I don't know how you feel, but I have no problem with what we're doing. We get rich, and our clients can brag about the great clinic they're going to. They'll be well satisfied and, actually, be better off for it. When I think about it, I often wonder just how much doctors are really doing. Much of what we do may have never been intended in the big scheme of things. We often prolong life and change the course of diseases. Is that what was really meant? Fifty years ago, a child that was born had about a one-in-one-hundred chance of being a diabetic. Today it is about one in ten because the genes have been kept in the population rather than being eliminated. A hundred years from now, doctors might be looked upon as the destroyers of the human race."

"Hey, I wouldn't be here if I didn't feel that way," Howie said, with dollar signs in his eyes.

"Me too," said Porky, adding that we seriously needed to get a bigger chair for the clubhouse.

We continued to talk nineteen to the dozen about our first day for a few hours over a couple of more beers, and Howie closed with his usual humor, "Better not let Lenny and Wayne know that the girls are sleeping over. Not that Jody would mind!"

I hit the sack late that night, exhausted. During the night, I had one of my lifelike dreams. The mystical voice, which I was familiar with, told me to be positive about everything and not to feel guilty. We were doing these patrons a favor. They would take pleasure in supporting such a worthy cause as ours. Astoundingly, this voice also told me to do routine immunoglobulin tests on the patients. The placebo effect of our exams and treatment and pleasure they derived from donating to us would surely increase their immunoglobulin levels. This would be excellent evidence of our beneficial treatment to any prospective onlookers. How I got these kinds of dreams is your guess as good as mine, but the advice never seemed to fail, so I did what the voice told me to. We did, to be sure, run these tests; and believe it or not, the immunoglobulin level rose significantly following our treatments. So I am convinced to this day that there was nothing wrong with what we did. Good fortune would befall us.

We were all fresh and ready to go at nine in the morning. Fortunately, the girls had all worn their uniforms, a bit wrinkled, for the final practice session. The weather had not let up. It was still bitter cold, and snow continued to accumulate. Tom, our groundskeeper, was doing his best to keep up with it, and Wayne was helping him. Several hours passed, and our first three appointments did not show up, not that we really expected them to. We were all apprehensively trying to look busy though there wasn't much to do. The girls were quizzing each other on their protocols and algorithms. When an answer was wrong or even slightly wrong, they took great delight in saying "Au contraire!" which they had recently absorbed from Porky. There were frequent smoke breaks.

Lo and behold! A little after noon, the security guard at the main gate called and said that he was escorting in our very first patient. It would turn out that he would be our only patient that day, but we were thankful for it. Everyone rushed to their stations. I asked Judy and Jody to stay up front so that it would look like we were well staffed. Regardless, I wanted them to see what was going on. I was listening in through the open door of my office as were the other two docs on their intercoms.

The security guard stated, "This is Mr. Randolph G. Remmington to see Dr. DeHaas."

"That is Randolph G. Remmington *the third!*" said Randy as we would call him when he was not present.

Randy was wearing sweatpants, a shirt that looked like it came from Goodwill, and gym shoes. However, he wore a very expensive, genuine sealskin parka over this (as he would let us know). It was not unusual for these wealthy men to dress in a down-to-earth manner. Most of them did not want special attention. He was well built for a man of sixty-two. He wore wire-rimmed glasses with a hearing aid attached. He was cheerful in his attitude and maintained a pleasant smile.

He shook hands with Rosy. "I am Randolph G. Remmington the third, and I am here to see Dr. DeHaas. Mr. Goldbergerstein recommended him. I flew in on my little Cessna yesterday from Cambridge, Massachusetts. Somehow I was able to land and get a decent suite at the Lakeside Inn. I would have flown in my private jet, but because of the weather, it wouldn't have been able to land. Besides, I like to pilot myself, and I need a pro to fly that monstrosity of a jet. That prep for the reaming was a real joy. Looking forward to a real meal." He liked to flaunt his wealth, which many of our clients would do, and this was always a good sign.

Rosy replied, "We all know how miserable those preps are, but unfortunately, they are a necessary evil." She then went through her rehearsed introduction and handed him the papers. He was impressed with how thorough we were. The forms were quite probing for obvious motives. Jody and Judy were looking busy going through files.

Rosy first sent Randy to Stephy who did his vital signs, performed pulmonary-function tests, and drew fasting blood samples. When she was done, she accompanied him to my office and, after helping him with a gown, told him that I would be there momentarily.

"Welcome to our humble clinic. I am Dr. DeHaas, and you are?"

Randy then went through his little narrative about his trip.

I was dressed in chic scrubs, which made him comfortable. "I see that you're from Massachusetts. Any relation to the famous Remmington?"

"Well, I am actually an heir. That's where most of my wealth came from. As you probably know, my great-great-grandfather founded one of the largest arms factories in the world. But I have nothing to do with the company other than inheritance. My source of wealth now is the greeting-card company, Happydays."

So I told Randy that we would have to get on with his history and examination. He smoked expensive cigars most of his life and had a benign tumor removed from his neck two years prior to his visit. This made him uneasy about cancer and was a chief reason he chose us. Other than that, he had a clean bill of past fitness. His examination was unremarkable other than a large scar on his anterior neck.

I then had to give him the bad news. "I'm sorry, Mr. Remmington, but our specialists were unable to make it in due to the severe weather. We'll have to postpone your stress test and colonoscopy to another date. I know you've been through that terrible prep, but I'm afraid you will have to go through it again at a later date. Because of the inconvenience, we'll pay for your trip."

I anticipated his response correctly. "That is not a problem. I like to fly. But that damn prep. I am not blaming you. I know it has to be done and would prefer it be done by an expert." In those days, they didn't put you to sleep for this procedure, so his concern was justifiable.

"We'll now get a chest film on you and then let you review it with Dr. Cranston. Let me introduce you to Helen, our X-ray technician. When you are done with everything, I'll see you again for a final briefing."

So I took him back to the X-ray room, and he met Helen. He was delighted with her and couldn't keep his eyes off her chest. She was so enticing, but he was very polite considering the age difference. She joked when she was ready to shoot the film. "This won't hurt a bit!"

Randy got dressed and then was taken to Howie's private office. Howie introduced himself and then put Randy's chest films up on the viewing board. He showed Randy where his heart and lungs were and simple things that a layman could understand. He then explained that everything looked perfectly normal which, of course, was a great relief to the pilot who smoked cigars. Howie then accompanied him back to my private office. I invited the other docs to sit in as we weren't very busy.

"Mr. Remmington, you have already met Dr. Cranston, our radiologist, and this is Dr. Schantz, our oncologist. Both have very impressive backgrounds and feel free to ask any questions of any one of us or all of us. We've found nothing unusual in anything we've done so far except some minor obstructive disease on your pulmonary-function test, which would be expected with your age and history of smoking. I want you to know that, though experimental at this stage, we feel that we have a complete cure for most types of cancer. This, as you may realize, is highly secretive at this stage for reasons that I need not explain. If you are found to have a type of cancer that we are dealing with, which includes most types, you are in the right place. Unfortunately, until these treatments become public, this is extremely expensive, and that is why we are forced at this time to offer it only to those who can afford it. Your exam is entirely free although we would appreciate any contribution to our worthy cause. However, because of our expenses, should you need treatment, we would have to charge for that. Insurance will not cover it because it is still regarded as experimental. But we'll talk about that further should the occasion arise. I know you've been fasting, and it's unfortunate we can't do that nasty test on you today, so you must be hungry and thirsty. As always, you will see that there is a selection of local cheeses, crackers, and the best wine in the world, Pink Catawba, grown and made right here. Please help yourself and tell us a little about yourself. Because of the weather, I would suggest that, when we're done here, we go over to our clubhouse where our excellent chef can fix you most anything you want. You're going to have to return in a few weeks to complete your tests, and we'd like to see you every six months or so to make sure everything is OK and to fill your routine prescriptions."

"It is a pleasure to meet all of you. I think you've answered any questions I might have had, so I have no questions. But I want you all to know that I am extremely impressed with what I see here. I want to at least leave a small token to show my gratitude. I'm going to tell all my friends about this place."

We went to the clubhouse for a gourmet dinner, which was called in before we left the clinic. Randy filled us in on his life history, schools he'd been to, and the joys of flying. When we were done, he took out his checkbook and wrote us a check for $15,000. He also paid for our meals. This was impressive to us, but it wouldn't have even been a penny on a dollar to you and me. But not a bad first day's work! We would need a lot more than that, however, to live in the style we longed for. How could we ever forget our first patient? After Randy left, we decided that, after the length of time that we took that day, we would limit our appointments to eight per day.

The following day, the snow eased, and two more patients who had been scheduled for the first day showed up. As the roads and airstrips cleared in the following weeks, we reached our goal of eight patients per day in about six weeks. They came from all over the world. Most of them flew in on their own planes, whether they were jets or cubs. We found that nearly every one of them were well mannered and enjoyed talking about themselves, which was fine with us. Most of them had a great sense of humor. You don't get that rich by being a grump. At least three-fourths of them dressed very casually—they liked to be looked upon as common folks. They all were very concerned about their well-being, or they wouldn't have been there. We never received a donation for less than $10,000. We made certain to put up donor plaques in our lobby to encourage larger donations. Lenny had underestimated the amounts that would be given. I am guessing that they now average about $20,000 per visit, not counting our charges for treatments. You must realize that this was a pittance to them. Almost to a one, they loved the recognition, and we were only too happy to comply.

It was sometime in May of that year that we felt comfortable enough with what we were doing to have our first patient for treatment. We would be careful to pick someone who met all our qualifications. He was escorted by the security guard to the clinic. Rosy went through her welcome speech. Stephy did his vital signs and pulmonary-function tests and drew blood. Chest X-rays were done by Helen. Our temporary cardiologist did a stress test. And finally, our gastroenterologist did his evil deed. He was treated to the usual snacks and Pink Catawba and then brought to my office. I had reviewed all his tests except for the blood tests, which would be sent out. All was hunky-dory. I introduced myself, and then he introduced himself.

"I'm very glad to meet you. You are almost too meticulous here. How impressive! My name is Ian McGraw, but please call me Red. You won't believe this, but I just sailed in yesterday on my sixty-eight-footer [they liked footage!] from New Orleans, the Big Easy. I have a little fishing fleet there."

I interrupted, "How in the world do you get here from New Orleans on a boat?"

"Easy, just sail around Florida on the intercoastal waterway, come up the Saint Lawrence Seaway, up the locks, and here I am. Those icebreakers do a great job. Had a great time."

"Wow!" I came to the point, "Red, I have some not-so-good news and some good news for you. Dr. Cranston, our radiologist, points out that you have something showing on your lung, and he'll show it to you and discuss it with you. It is probably malignant, but we'll do a bronchoscopy, where we look down into your lung and do a biopsy, just to make sure. The good news is that, if it is cancer, we have a virtual 100 percent cure that is available nowhere else. It is considered experimental, but we are having astounding results. We can do your bronchoscopy in our procedure room tomorrow. I know this has got to be causing you a great deal of anxiety, and I'll be pleased to prescribe something for you if you wish." I surprised myself in that I had no trouble telling him this. I had rehearsed it time and again.

Red was, as you would expect, a redheaded Irishman. Even his face was red. He had a prominent beer belly. Bragging was his forte. He gave a horrible grimace when he was presented with the news, but he readily became very serious and attentive. We had a procedure room where we could administer IV anesthesia and do minor surgery or invasive procedures if needed. We actually had no bronchoscope (they were expensive), but come on, they'd be asleep. Remember—no harm! After he got dressed, I took him to meet Howie in his viewing room. Howie had dug out an appropriate film that any idiot could see was abnormal. He would put Red's actual film alongside to show what a normal chest X-ray looked like. He went through a similar dialogue to mine and informed Red that Dr. Schantz would discuss treatment with him after he examined the tissue, which was nonexistent, microscopically. Howie too explained to us later how effortless this was. He had told Red to try to keep all of this to himself, knowing that Red would tell all his colleagues of his miraculous cure.

Red returned the following morning and had his bronchoscopy. After he recovered from his deep sleep, he was shown to Porky's office.

"I am Dr. Schantz, an oncologist, and I will be in charge of your treatment. I've examined your specimen and, indeed, it shows a malignant process going on. First and foremost, I want you to know that the treatment is completely painless. It will require some short stays in our professionally staffed inpatient department, twelve intravenous treatments in all. We'll also treat you with our one-of-a-kind emission machine, the NNI. The plus about all of this is that we have obtained nothing but complete cures with our treatment. The disadvantage is that the treatment is exceedingly expensive, and only people like yourself can afford it. We hope this will change once it becomes acceptable to the medical establishment. You'll stay in a suite complete with phone, TV, shower, and Jacuzzi. You can eat anything you want, but it will be required that you eat one-and-one-half cups of asparagus every day throughout your treatment. That is needed to augment the medication you will be getting. It is necessary that we charge for this treatment because there is no other way we could cover expenses. Get ready for a shock! The five NNI treatments will cost $30,000 each. The twelve IV treatments will cost $41,250 each [a realistic figure]. I can almost guarantee you that you will not get results like ours anywhere else. If you prefer not to be treated [Yeah, sure!], we accept your decision. I would suggest we start your first treatment tomorrow and daily after that. Do you have any problem with any of this?"

"I love asparagus!"

A cool half million! Now we're talking cancer! Red was delighted with his room and service. Jody and Judy were thrilled to have their first patient. The IVs were "prepared" by Porky with technical labels on them so that the nurses were not aware of what they were giving, but they were warned that the patient might pee frequently and pee blue. Howie would treat him with the advanced blender—on, off, on, off. After two months, Red would return, and a repeat film would show that the tumor had completely disappeared. He was advised to return yearly because, after all, this was experimental; and there could be a recurrence. If he were really ever to come down with cancer, we would tell him that it would not be advisable that we continue to treat him; and we would refer him to a famous cancer clinic in Houston, which, indeed, was doing real experimental work. He tipped each of the girls $500. He would, as we predicted, tell his filthy-rich friends of his mind-blowing cure.

As time went on, we would cautiously handpick clients for cures. We limited them to about one per day and never had more than five inpatients at a time, other than during the tornado, which you will be told about. Aware that they would not listen to us about discretion, the patients invariably told all their friends of their wonderful remedy. Within six months, we had so much demand that we began to select only the wealthiest of the wealthy, based on their background checks, which Lenny did. We were all becoming multimillionaires. Not the girls, of course, but they kept getting substantial raises that were well ahead of their respective fields. They were advised by Lenny not to parade their good fortune as others might want their positions. We were cleansing the wealthy of cancer and also some of their surplus cash. We tried to return some of our wealth to good old Harry, but he was so impressed with what we were doing that he wanted us to expand. We told him that it was too early to know the final results, but he insisted on throwing in another ten million dollars for exploring this possibility. He had collected a nice sum from Vermilion Estates. Who were we to deny him the pleasure of a charitable contribution? Lenny knew all the legal loopholes to funnel the money back to us just as many charities do. Everyone, including the girls, felt that we had earned every penny of it.

Summer came, and Trixie arrived at the beginning of July. Lenny, Wayne, and all three docs were present for her initial evaluation. Who could miss that? She knew fully well what her job would be. Wayne had filled her in on that. She looked even sexier in her expensive outfit than I could remember when she just wore a bikini. Maybe I was just getting older! She was elfin in stature but very well assembled. The only piercings were in her earlobes. She appeared to have no makeup on though I'm sure she knew how to handle that too. Her loose, see-through blouse showed plenty of cleavage. She wore half-length denims. She knew all the right moves and spoke with a soft, enticing voice.

Taking it all in, I spoke, "I guess you and all of us know what you're here for. You'll be well paid, so no screwing up, pardon the pun. No fraternizing with any of the employees. As you know, you'll be expected to do favors for visitors. You'll be housed on Lenny's yacht and well cared for. We don't expect you to be subjected to anything risky. If you feel that you are being abused, the captain has agreed to intervene. You'll be tested monthly for venereal diseases. So everything should be lots of fun for you. Absolutely no drugs and no excessive drinking. Get the idea?"

"I get the picture. A shame I can't take care of some of you guys, though. I love the taste of that stuff!"

Porky tuned in, "Of course, you're just joking." We all knew she wasn't. To my knowledge, none of the employees ever had any intimate contact with her. But I can be quite naive at times. A pleasant time was had by many of our patients aboard Lenny's yacht that summer. Trixie acted like quite a lady during off-hours and never caused anyone any trouble. She often accompanied visitors to local attractions like Cedar Point, Kelly's Island, Tony Packo's (a famous Hungarian hot dog place in Toledo), and not to be omitted, the legendary Blue Hole in nearby Castalia. I had been to the Blue Hole myself as a kid and during my investigation into the area. It is really nothing but just that, a blue hole. It is a very azure little pond, supposedly bottomless. In fact, it's somewhat boring. But it does have beautiful gardens. There was, in reality, a lot to do in that area. And the German and Italian restaurants are something that no one should ignore.

Matters went favorably for all through the first year of our existence. There was never any question in any of our minds that we were doing anything but good for our patients. We were making certain that they were healthy and making them better human beings. That we were getting prosperous from it was merely a pleasant circumstance and was to everyone's benefit. We were bringing in a lot of outside money, so the local politicians were very supportive.

Surely, everyone was happy and wealthy, and no one would get hurt.

CHAPTER SEVEN

The Inspectors Cometh

The first year of business was successful beyond my expectations. The patients, employees, local politicians, and even the part-time help were well satisfied and had no complaints.

On February 1, 1996, one year to the date from our opening, Rosy called my office and told me that a government employee was on the phone. I had her transfer the call back to my office. It was an administrator from OSHA (Occupational Safety and Health Administration). I had been anticipating a call from them. The predator advised me that they would have three inspectors visit our facility on July 6. I had had prior experience with these idiots and knew that it was customary for them to give several months' notice. Every hospital I was with knew a year in advance. So much for surprise inspections! Lenny had reviewed all the OSHA policies, and we felt that we were totally compliant, but we would do whatever last-minute sprucing up that had to be done.

Hospitals actually appoint special committees for this purpose. I've never known any place to get perfect grades, if you might call them that. There are major infractions and minor infractions. Major infractions were always granted a six-month correctional period, at which time they would be reinspected. Certificates were given for passing inspections. These inspectors are all underpaid, so they thrive on perks like travel pay and offerings. I imagine there might be a very few who take their job seriously, so we had to prepare for that event. There were special clauses that applied to experimental work so as to protect the researchers from intellectual theft. I would take full advantages of these protective regulations. We would lighten our patient load during the three or four days they were there. Porky would do most of the talking since he had the most free time. Porky, Howie, and I had frequent meetings to make sure that we were all in line with each other.

On the morning of July 6, security called to let us know that three OSHA inspectors were at our main gate. Security had been instructed to make sure that they had all the proper identification papers.

Rosy greeted them with her prepared speech, "You must be the OSHA inspectors that we have been looking forward to. My name is Rosy. I'll get Dr. DeHaas when he is through with his patient. If you would be so kind as to show me your identification and introduce yourselves, I will tell him your names."

We purposely made them wait forty-five minutes to give the impression of thoroughness and to give them ample opportunity to view all our documents in the lobby, some of which were required by law. I can't remember their names, but behind their backs, we would call them "Letcher, Treacher, and Fetcher" at Howie's suggestion. So that's how I'll refer to them. The names fit them very well.

Letcher appeared to be about forty. He wore a suit and tie as did all of them—the typical official government-looking suits. There were some small old food stains on his suit jacket. He wore a bright tie with large flowers on it. He wore a Rolex watch, which I'm certain was fake. He carried a briefcase and legal pad that was mounted on a clipboard. He spent most of his time inspecting every inch of our girls and showed no shame in exhibiting his glare. He would love Trixie!

Treacher was a sneaky-looking little fellow that might have been Hitler's twin. He combed his hair much like Hitler and had a mustache that was similar. He kept looking over his shoulder and fiddling with his mustache. There were wire-rimmed glasses with little, teeny lenses perched on his nose. He too carried a briefcase, but one with a huge OSHA decal on it. This guy could be trouble.

Fetcher was your typical gofer redneck. He was short and stocky. His face was indeed red. His mouth took up half of his face. He spoke in a deep voice with a West Virginia accent. He looked out of place in a suit. Anytime that Letcher and Treacher would say something, he would say, "I'll second that!" Not too bright, but who said that was a qualification?

"Hello, I am Dr. DeHaas. Welcome to our humble facility [they liked that term]. If it pleases you, I would like to take you on a tour, and then you may be free to do what you have to do. I know you all must be tired from your trip from Las Vegas. May I suggest that, when you are done today, we have lunch at our clubhouse, and you might like to stay on our attorney's yacht while you are here. You might enjoy perch-fishing at Put-In-Bay. I would be pleased to answer any of your questions, and Dr. Schantz and Dr. Cranston will spend more time with you. I understand that we are under the experimental guidelines. If there are no questions, let's get started."

Fetcher smirked. "I'll second that!"

I proceeded to show the three agents our beautiful facility. I introduced them to all our girls, and they could not hide their leers. They would save their inspection for a time when they were alone. When we arrived at Howie's office, I turned them over to him. Howie was well versed on the experimental phrases in the rules. He explained his office and displayed a few films showing some of our miraculous cures. He showed them the regular X-ray room and explained how the lead lining met specifications. He pointed to Helen to show that she was wearing her radiation tag, but they weren't looking at the tag with their goggle-eyed expressions.

Letcher spoke, "We'd like to see your experimental equipment."

Howie responded, "I'm sure you are well aware that, under your own guidelines, I am not required to demonstrate our negative-neutron ionizer as it is a research tool in progress. It is kept in a top secret locked room. I'll show it to you but can't run it in your presence."

"I've never heard of a negative neutron," replied Treacher with an erudite air.

"Well now, we may know something that isn't in the books yet."

"I'll second that!", piped Fetcher.

We had planned to have Porky do most of the talking, but they were tired from their trip from Las Vegas, so their conversation was cut short. Anyone could see that they were anxious for their wining and dining. We would have a rough time outdoing Sin City, but we would give it our best shot. At the midday meal, they met Lenny and Wayne. Treacher let Lenny know that the next day would be spent with him going over policies and financial records. The other docs and I were confident that Lenny had everything on the up-and-up. Lenny, Wayne, Letcher, and Treacher had lobster with Pink Catawba and all the trimmings; Howie had the local perch; Porky, like a good boy, had a Greek salad (he was down to 250 pounds by this time); Fletcher had the West Virginia favorite—slaw dogs, fries, and beer; and I had my usual grilled cheese and Gift Wasser. There was absolutely no discussion about the clinic.

Following our sumptuous lunch, the three stooges were escorted to Lenny's yacht by our security. There they were treated to hors d'oeuvres and introduced to the captain who suggested late-evening perch fishing off Big Bass Island. And of course, Trixie was there to greet them in her itsy-bitsy, teensy-weensy yellow polka-dot bikini. We heard through the grapevine the following morning that all three of them were treated to every human depravity possible.

After their first gratifying night, they showed up at Lenny's office at about 11:00 AM

"What a fantastic night," said Letcher. "We caught plenty of perch. Hope we didn't catch anything else!"

Again from Fetcher, "I'll second that!"

They spent all of one hour skimming through this and that with Lenny. Lenny did a great job using his indecipherable legalese to show where money went. We were all, as it should be, millionaires by now. Fifty thousand dollars was now considered a slow day. We all knew that Lenny was overpaying himself, and he knew that we knew. But nobody said anything about it because we were happy to have him as our keeper. Large personal items were purchased through the organization legitimately. The girls now had their own company cars. On and on.

Needless to say, they were eager to return to the boat or "ship" as Lenny insisted on calling it. Lenny had originally named it *Serenity* but had recently registered it as *Trixie's Delight*. So by 2:00 PM, they were back on the craft. Trixie had great energy and never seemed to wear out. She loved to put on her short shorts and see-through blouse and go to the Blue Hole (which was terribly boring to most), but they would please her so she could please them.

The third day that they were there was spent going unsupervised through the clinic, looking for such things as fire exits, bottles under sinks, and other such trifling things. Probably most of their time was spent gawking at the girls. Letcher had asked me privately if Helen were available, but I told him, "Hands off!"

Another night of ecstasy was had; and in the morning of the fourth day, when they were ready to leave, Letcher spoke, "It appears to us that you have a fine facility here. We found a few minor infractions such as handling of some possibly dangerous disposables and a couple of your girls with hair length beyond the standard, but these are entirely correctable, and we would expect to see results on our next yearly visit. We all had a very pleasant time and hope to see you again next year. You should get your superior approval certificate within two weeks. Law requires that you display it in a prominent place."

I felt like saying "How about on Trixie's boobs?" but kept my mouth shut. We expected some ridiculous violations as they had to show their supervisors that they had done something.

They parted with jovial good-byes. Our mission was a success. They had spent very little time doing the job the taxpayers had shelled out to do. Jody and Stephy would have to put their hair up in buns while they were working—not a problem. Not surprisingly, we would see Letcher, Treacher, and Fetcher annually.

Everyone was happy and wealthy and no harm had come to anyone. The old adage—do no harm!

"I'll second that!"

CHAPTER EIGHT

Disaster Strikes

It wouldn't surprise me that after you read the title of this chapter, you were thinking of a different kind of disaster. No, this was a genuine, natural disaster.

In early July of 1997, there were severe storms throughout Northern Ohio. These came at a particularly bad time because many were getting ready for the Fourth of July celebration. Shops were full of people, and the roads along Lake Erie's shore were jammed with traffic. This area had a reputation for severe storms during the summer and was known as Tornado Alley. Any old-timer will remember the record number of tornadoes that hit in and around Sandusky on a line to Lorain on July 2.

All our personnel along with three inpatients and four outpatients were present in our clinic building that morning at about 9:00 AM. There were no early satellite warnings such as we have today. Howie had gone outside for some fresh air and a cigarette. When he came in, he said, "Man, those skies are getting darker than the dark side of the moon." And sure enough, within ten minutes, golf-ball-sized hail was coming down, and the winds picked up considerably. Wayne had constructed our clinic building with double-brick thickness to withstand most storms, so we felt pretty safe.

Then we could see the funnel cloud approaching Vermilion Estates. Shingles started to fly and then beams and telephone poles. For sake of sounding trite, words cannot describe it. It really sounded like a freight train. It was amazing how the vortex could destroy a rather solid building and leave a wooden storage barn right next to it untouched.

Our clinic was largely spared. The only damage to it was a large maple tree toppled on the roof. After only minutes, the storm passed and we all went outside where it was deathly silent. We walked over to the estates to survey the damage. About ten of the mansions were nearly completely leveled, and there was significant damage to most of them. Debris was everywhere as were former occupants crying for help. Electricity was out in an extensive area. Luckily we had, by law, backup generators for our clinic. The local water tower was spared, so we had water.

We had all had disaster training and went immediately to work. Tom, Wayne, and Lenny transported a number of injured to the clinic on detached doors. Being a research facility, we had limited supplies but were able to do basic things such as stopping the bleeding, suturing, and applying splints. The surrounding hospitals were overwhelmed with injured and a few dying patients, so the local police and fire departments called us to see if we could help. I informed them that we had X-ray capability and asked them if they could bring us some supplies. I told them that we could take a limited number of minor injuries and they could transport them to our clinic where we could treat them to take some of the load off the hospitals. Having had training in emergency medicine and disaster training, I left Howie and Porky, our two rent-a-docs, and our nurses and technicians to go to Sandusky General to help with the more serious stuff. I first stopped by home to make sure Connie was OK.

Connie had tears streaming down her face. "We really lucked out. Our little employee complex had almost no damage. But what about the others? You go do what you have to do."

This was not a time for one of Connie's cute little games, so I headed straight for the hospital. There I did triage on the incoming patients, sending them off in appropriate directions and caring for the minor injuries. This may sound trivial to the layman, but in disasters, the most experienced person should be in charge of triage. I can remember that one fellow had a perforated abdomen and blood was gushing out. I had reached in and put a clamp on his splenic artery until he could get to surgery. Never did find out what happened to him.

As it turned out, there were over six hundred injuries and three deaths attributed to the tornadoes. Castalia and Huron were hit particularly hard, but damage was widespread. After things settled down, the hospital administrator came down to personally thank me and invited me to become a member of the staff. I told him, however, that I had more important things to tend to.

Most of the homeowners at Vermilion Estates had no insurance because they were filthy rich and nearly all astute entrepreneurs and knew insurance was statistically a bad bet. Some of them actually had their own insurance companies. All were anxious to build an even larger and more elegant manor. Of course, Wayne and Tom were extremely pleased about this. When I informed

Howie that there was no damage to his house, he responded, "As you slide down the banister of life, may the splinters never point the wrong way!"

The mayor, Guido Franco, came out to our clinic with his entourage of American-Italian and American-German politicians to give us a citation plaque. And of course, the local newspapers and TV stations were there to get pictures of their ugly faces. Howie commented afterward, "Diapers and politicians should be changed often for the same reason!" The local police and fire departments both gave us citations of heroism, which were placed along with the many other documentations in our lobby. But that was as it should be, considering we made annual contributions of $10,000 to both. It was pleasant to see all the Italians and Germans working as one during that crisis, but it was not long before it was politics as usual. Lenny had used a little-known ruling called charitable distribution, where one charity may give to another to avoid tax or legal problems with our contributions.

Wayne and Tom went immediately to work repairing the estates and building new mansions. Fourteen new estates were added, bringing the total now to sixty-two. Tom's barn and equipment were miraculously untouched by the storm, so he and his crew were at work that very day with chain saws and bulldozers. We thanked Wayne for his foresight in building a sturdy clinic for us. The regional politicos were extremely pleased to see the additional real estate taxes coming in. We actually made a profit of something over four million dollars with the new estates and rebuilding. Within fifteen months, all was pristine again, except for the loss of a number of large primordial trees (which a lumber company actually paid us for).

Fortunately, there were only about ten minor injuries and no deaths to the residents of Vermilion Estates. We had taken care of most of those, right in our clinic. We were all looked upon as heroes by the local populace.

We had to cancel our appointments for one week but were right back at it the following week.

So once again, everyone was happy and wealthy with only some minor, unforeseen injuries!

CHAPTER NINE

An Unlikely Tryst

Because of the damage and heartache from the storm in 1997, the Christmas party that year was quite subdued and solemn. Everyone received their bonuses, but planned entertainment was eliminated except for carols from a local chorus group. All present were told that we would more than make up for it the following holiday season. There were no complaints.

We did, indeed, make up for it at the Christmas party of 1998. The clubhouse had been redecorated by Wayne and was larger than before and was again the ideal place for our annual bash. There was now a professional performing stage in this building with a nightclub setting.

Big-name stars, names who I won't reveal, were on hand to perform. Local dignitaries were present with their spouses or friends. Several of our more-trusted patients were there. Harry Thorndike, guest of honor, sat in the middle of the front table; and one of the stars dedicated a song written just for him. A few of the residents from the estates were also present. There were even a few Arabs there. Porky had suggested that we invite Letcher, Treacher, and Fetcher; but Lenny prudently advised that was not a wise thing to do. Our New Year's party, also held at the clubhouse, was a private affair just for the employees and their families. It was more traditional.

Alcohol flowed freely, and a few of the younger women jumped nude into the indoor swimming pool to loud cheers from the onlookers. The buffet was complete with ice carvings, lobster, and prime rib. Seasonal flowers decorated every table. There was a separate, well-ventilated area for smokers, which was actually unlawful but was tolerated just for this event by the local fire and police departments. After all, we had been giving them each $10,000 every year in appreciation of their services. We also sponsored a lavish Christmas party for youngsters every year at the yacht club.

All our employees had been present every year for the parties. Even Trixie came this year. She behaved like a perfect lady—even wore her bra and panties when she jumped in the pool. However, in 1998, two were notably missing for the Christmas and New Year parties. Howie and Jody were nowhere to be seen. It appeared that absolutely no one knew where they were. This was very strange as this was the most extravagant event yet. How could anyone miss something like this?

When our business hours resumed on January 5, 1999, Howie and Jody both showed up for work on time, beaming from ear to ear. Jody chose not to talk about her absence to anyone.

I took Howie aside in my private room. "Howie, where he hell were you for the holidays?"

"I just needed to get out of this godforsaken weather. Headed down to New Orleans. What a great city! They call it the Big Easy down there."

"You went with Jody, didn't you? I thought we had all agreed that there would be no intimate relations with the employees."

"Come on, Fast Eddy, I don't tell you how to run your life. We just had a good time. That's all."

"Well, I guess there was no harm done. You two are the talk of the clinic though."

So everyone went about business as usual, except for the fact that Jody hung around Howie's office during all her free time, and she didn't wear quite so much makeup. He certainly established that he was not gay as some had suspected.

Even though Jody was very close to her sister, Judy, nothing, to my knowledge, was ever revealed about the events of the New Orleans trip. Nonetheless, about six weeks after her return, Jody began to take on a pregnant stature with her slightly swollen belly and enlarging breasts. She could no longer hide it.

When it became apparent that everyone was aware of the expectant condition in late February, Howie and Jody announced to everyone that they were getting married.

This time, I invited both Howie and Jody to my private room.

"Well, it appears you two are madly—or may I say insanely—in love. I think you are both going to be very happy with each other. Your personalities fit well. I have talked it over with Lenny, Porky, and Wayne. We would like to treat you both to a wedding that will be remembered by all. We could have it at the clubhouse. How do you two feel about that?"

They looked at each other and smiled. In unison, they said, "We love you, Fast Eddy!" The date was set for the first Saturday in June. Jody had already moved in with Howie, and they were preparing a room for the new arrival.

I never once heard any mention from anyone about their significant age difference. We all just saw how happy they were with each other.

During the next few months, all the employees joined in to help plan the coming event. Good old Harry bought an elegant wedding ring from Tiffany's for Howie to present to Jody. The girls had a very expensive white dress designed, which would hide the obvious. Judy, of course, would be the bridesmaid. Howie wanted me to be the best man, but I talked him into having Harry as he was the one who made all of this possible. Tom would supply the flowers, hopefully not eating any of them. Lenny suggested to them that he would do a prenuptial agreement, but they would have no part of that. He did revise their wills though.

As it turned out, the clubhouse was not even large enough to handle all the guests. All our employees, a number of our patients, many of the homeowners, most of the local government workers, the press, and others were invited to the wedding and reception. Because of the huge number of people, we decided to hold the wedding outside and do the banquet inside. A popular band was brought up from Las Vegas. Expense was not a problem. Besides, we would get great, positive publicity from this. Personally, I did not want all the publicity. But Howie, Wayne, Porky, and Lenny were all eager to expand; so I was outvoted on the publicity part.

The grand day came. Morning was spent getting the bride and groom looking like a king and queen. Wayne and Tom were busy giving the grounds their final touches. A graceful trellis was built for the final nuptial. Off duty police provided the extra security we would need. The fire department had a huge ladder truck on hand to blow the siren after the ceremony. Our chef was complaining about the effect of the heat on his ice carvings. The minister and mayor were joining forces to prepare a unique rite. A mammoth cake was delivered from a neighborhood Italian restaurant. The German restaurants and wineries donated their finest alcoholic beverages.

As already stated, there was an unusual mix of people present. They arrived by their limousines driven by their chauffeurs. It was a good thing that most arrived with drivers because there was not enough parking space, and they wound up parking way down the road. Refreshments had to be sent out to the drivers. What was impressive was the many Arabs present in their native garbs. These guys really relished parties and gave very extravagant gifts. Howie and Jody would be set for the rest of their lives. Good old Harry never looked so regal. He treated them like a father. Indeed, the child would be named after him—Harry, not Harold. The women, because of the heat, were happy to show as much of their breasts as possible, much to the joy of the men.

The whole affair went perfectly. Never was such a loving kiss observed. At the reception, most became high on the generous gifts of alcohol. But security saw to it that nothing got out of hand. Not many could understand one another anyway because of all the different languages that were spoken. The reception went on all afternoon, and at dusk, we had a huge fireworks-display sponsored by the local politicians.

On Sunday, Howie and Jody were off on a two-week Mediterranean cruise that was a gift from Lenny, Wayne, and Tom. When they returned, it was work as usual. Jody worked right up to the day of her delivery, about seven months later. She actually left right from work to go to the hospital. A beautiful baby Harry was brought to life.

I really doubt that Howie has ever told Jody the true nature of his job. For all she knows, he is a god who can cure cancer. Never know what goes on behind closed doors though.

CHAPTER TEN

A Fitting End

It was the year 2002. All had gone well through nearly a decade of our existence.

The Vermilion Estates continued to thrive and expand. There were now ninety-six homeowners. Nearly half of them were Arabs—sheiks and whatnot. Friendly people that kept to themselves. Background checks had been made on all homeowners in an attempt to thwart any criminal activity. The clubhouse was enlarged and now included a six-lane bowling alley. The golf course, thanks to Wayne and Tom, was expanded to eighteen professionally designed holes. Trixie played the nineteenth hole on special occasions.

Harold Thorndike, or good old Harry, was killed the prior year when lightning struck him on the Brookshire golf course. There must have been over a thousand mourners at his funeral. I'm sure that many of them were awaiting the reading of his will. I made certain that his tombstone read Harry Thorndike and not Harold. I'm sure he would have wanted this.

Leonard Goldbergerstein, or Lenny, continued as the keeper of our finances. He now had a secretary who had no access to the records. Lenny became an expert on charitable law and traveled and sailed the world, giving lectures on the subject. He sometimes took his cute little secretary with him. He now had a 134-foot yacht and would have had a larger one if not for the docking space at Vermilion Harbor. His tic became worse and worse as he aged, and he was nearly unbearable to be around. He wanted to try our negative-neutron ionizer, but Howie assured him that it wouldn't help. Lenny was very impressed with the number of cures we had.

Wayne continued to improve the estates and spent much time running around with Lenny. His ex-wife was now coming after him for more child support. He was paying $100,000 per year for each of his two kids, and Lenny made sure that amount was plenty. No need to spoil the children. Wayne spent a lot of time at the tennis courts, instructing and using many of the tricks I had taught him in the past. He was overwhelmingly sought after by the wealthy young women at the clubhouse, and I'm sure he had no need of Trixie's services.

Howie and Jody settled in at the estates after their marriage and now had three spoiled brats. I know now that he certainly wasn't gay. He still stacked his beer cans and even called Jody a bush. And he still came up with his corny phrases and occasionally sang his version of "Walk Right In." He basically liked to do nothing and had hired help for everything.

Tomas Strausser, or Tom, spent all his spare time at his barn. We did all we could to keep him from accumulating junk, but it was beginning to pile up again although I will admit it was a higher quality of junk. So we just had a high-rise fence built around it to hide it from view. He was a genius when it came to nature and invented a number of devices to raise chickens, rabbits, and pigs with a minimum of effort. He was, of course, very rich by now and spent much of his time searching for properties with rare trees. He knew every tree by common and scientific names. He would buy the land, sell the trees to lumber companies, and resell the land, making huge profits. More power to him. He continued to look like your common hermit.

Dr. John Schantz, or Porky, which everyone now called him even to his face, enjoyed his family life and spent most of his time at home. He had become a health nut and was now down to a respectable 210 pounds but was still called Porky. He was much more jovial now that he found some purpose in life. Unfortunately, he liked to gamble and would go to frequent "seminars" in Las Vegas and Atlantic City. He seemed always in need of money even though he was making millions. But everyone has their problems.

Rosy continued at the front desk. She was now separated from her husband and going through marriage counseling. Seems there was a problem with her making more than her husband. She, however, remained cheerful and professional at work.

Helen, our cute little X-ray tech, was offered a position in Hollywood as a TV star in a series that you are all familiar with. One of our patients, a producer of a large movie company, convinced her to go out to Hollywood with him. She left us in 2000 and was replaced by another cute little novice tech. When she left, she told Howie, "I've found a new position." Howie returned, "Great, let's try it!"

Stephanie Dickenson, or Stephy, continued in her role and only became more attractive as she matured. She was great at work. Her main problem at that time was that she was shacked up with the very male nurse we had rejected. Needless to say, he didn't show up at our lavish Christmas and Fourth of July parties.

Judy was still with us and loved working with her rich, newly married sister. She still lived with her live-in boyfriend who now had advanced muscular dystrophy. She spent all her extra time caring for him. Greater love was never had.

Trixie, I believe, was worn out in more ways than one. She left us in 1999, and we never heard from her again. Occasionally, though, we heard stories about Trixie from patients who came from all over the world. She apparently did favorable advertising for us. She was replaced through a madam from the Happy Homestead Ranch in Vegas that Wayne was familiar with. Our new girl was called Ringa Belle and proved very adequate. She rang many bells!

Our clinic became overwhelmed with requests by prospective patients. Over half of our patients were now Arabs from many Middle East countries. As Howie said, "Lemon, Serious, Tuna Sandwich, and Jordache!" Dumb, but true! None of us actually had any prejudice whatsoever due to our prior professional and military experience. For some reason, these Arabs wanted to live forever even though they had thousands of virgins awaiting them upon their demise. We had all tried in vain to counsel them on their obesity, but what would you do if you were allowed to eat any exotic food any time you wanted to? One emir had very little incentive to lose weight as he taxed his tribe his weight in gold every year. But to get back to the point, Howie, Lenny, Porky, and Wayne wanted to open more research centers. I was happy with what we had. Of course, Lenny and Wayne were impressed with our miraculous cures and believed it was now time to offer it to the public in general. On the other hand, Howie and Porky were impressed mainly with the money, and all of us docs knew that there were plenty of other disgruntled physicians out there ready to jump in. We all certainly knew how to generate cash to open new facilities. So in July 2002, we planned an administrative meeting to discuss our future.

Therefore, I would first discuss things with Connie. I asked her, "Do you ever think about what your life would be like if we had never met?" She responded, "Ever since we met!" Of course, it was meant in fun. I told her that I had accomplished everything that I dreamed of doing. Our worth was now over ten million dollars after taxes. There was no need for any more money. Our kids had everything they needed and were doing well, and large monetary gifts would just spoil them. They could wait until we were gone. I told her that I was tired of working and wanted to enjoy myself traveling and doing things that I hadn't had time for.

"But look at all the good you've done for so many people. Besides, you'll be a pain in the butt being around here all the time."

"The work will go on without me. And I have plenty of things to keep me busy so that I won't be in your hair."

I rarely won arguments with Connie, but she realized that I had provided her with a very enjoyable life. She reluctantly told me to do what I thought was right.

I had been working on a theory that, again, was brought to my mind by that strange, supernatural voice in my dreams that was never wrong. Perhaps Einstein was similarly inspired. I was familiar with recent stem-cell research. This power told me that stem cells did not inherently recognize what organ they were about to become. Instead, the structure created by their division created anatomic tissues and organs based on need. This was contrary to the conventional wisdom at that time, but made sense. It needed working on and could, indeed, lead to many cures and treatment of suffering.

Hence we had our meeting the following week. I started. "You guys can do what you wish, but I am just too worn out to get involved in a big expansion. You should have no problem finding some miserable bastard to replace me." I went on to tell them about my stem-cell theory, and they thought it was a great idea that should be incorporated into our "research," but for real. Exploration into my theory continues to this day.

Lenny spoke up, "We'll be sorry to see you leave us, Dr. Ed. You've done a wonderful job putting this all together, and we will all be forever grateful to you. The four of us want to open up more clinics. I, for one, would like to see your treatments become available to everyone. A number of our rent-a-docs are obviously very dissatisfied with what they are doing at other places, and I am sure Dr. Cranston and Dr. Schantz can convince them to be in charge of new research facilities. I think, in gratitude to Mr. Thorndike, that we should retain his name on these new establishments."

"I'll second that," said Howie, "But we are not yet at a point where we can make this affordable for everyone. We have a huge backlog of very wealthy patients, though, to sustain new clinics."

So we all parted on very friendly terms. They would go on to open up five new clinics with a similar format. There was no trouble whatsoever finding discontented doctors to work in the clinics. We were all beginning to wonder if there were any doctors at all that were satisfied with their working conditions and government regulations. Professional decisions were rapidly being replaced by the whims of novices and money-mongers. All the clinics were in communities similar to Vermilion, maybe one near you. Each clinic had planned homeowner estates similar to ours, providing support and security. Lenny would continue to manage my taxes for me. He suggested that each of us invest a couple of million dollars in silver US coins to protect against hard times—good advice as these have increased ten times in value.

The twist to this account is that there is no twist. Everyone, including our patients, the politicians, the inspectors, and good old Harry (God bless him!), continues to be happy and wealthy. No one has ever been hurt. Au contraire, it was now a status symbol to be a patient or to even be associated with our organization.

We all became rich beyond our wildest dreams. I was happy to get out at about ten million dollars, but the others would go on to accumulate much greater wealth. Porky lost most of his money gambling but kept enough to support his family in grand style—I am not his judge. I'm sure he made plenty of people in Sin City happy.

Connie and I chose to move to Canton, Ohio, so that she could be close to her daughters. We live in a modest house in an inconspicuous neighborhood. Neither of us wanted the upkeep of a mansion. There are a lot of great activities in and around Canton. Connie had grown up there and is active in her Lehman High (now defunct) alumni. The first question that everyone asks you in Canton is, of all things, "What high school did you go to?" Drives me nuts—who cares what high school you went to? The high school football teams there draw more than some professional teams. Insane! But otherwise, a great community.

We still go to the annual Christmas and Fourth of July parties up in Vermilion. We have big-name stars for singing and music. Our fireworks dwarf Cedar Point's. Even Helen, now a famous movie star, comes to our events. Reporters try to get in, but our security is tight.

The winters are ruthless in Northern Ohio, so Connie and I try to get to warm climes as much as possible. She likes to enjoy the holidays with the kids and grandkids. She still devises her bedtime games, but not nearly so often. I stay out of her hair except for those times.

I spend my time doing watercolors, watching the Indians, going to the local euchre club once a week, doing inconsequential chores around the house, and now writing. I get exceptional medical care from the VA because of my Purple Heart. I feel like I've done it all.

As they said on *The Sonny & Cher Comedy Hour*, the beat goes on!

Edwards Brothers, Inc.
Thorofare, NJ USA
October 3, 2011